She felt useless. Like he thought she was nothing but some frightened waste of space.

A liability.

“I never should’ve put you in this position,” Zack said. “You’re hardly trained for any of this. Just swim back to shore, and I’ll figure out what we’re going to do from here.”

Rebecca took a deep breath and felt the comfort of air filling her lungs. Then she dived down again.

She could hear the distorted sound of Zack shouting echo above the water. She didn’t stop. She didn’t need to hear what he was saying. The look on his face had been clear. Zack thought she was some awkward klutz who’d flailed around foolishly, made the truck sink and cost him their only chance at recovering the stolen material.

Zack and Seth might be fighting on different sides of a battle, but their opinion of her seemed to be the same. She was going to prove them both wrong.

Maggie K. Black is an award-winning journalist and romantic suspense author with an insatiable love of traveling the world. She has lived in the American South, Europe and the Middle East. She now makes her home in Canada with her history teacher husband, their two beautiful girls and a small but mighty dog. Maggie enjoys connecting with her readers at maggiekblack.com.

Books by Maggie K. Black

Love Inspired Suspense

Killer Assignment
Deadline
Silent Hunter
Headline: Murder
Christmas Blackout
Tactical Rescue

Visit the Author Profile page at Harlequin.com.

Tactical Rescue

Maggie K. Black

LOVE INSPIRED BOOKS

ISBN-13: 978-0-373-67753-5

Tactical Rescue

This edition published by arrangement with Love Inspired Books.

www.Harlequin.com

Printed in U.S.A.

If we are thrown into the blazing furnace,
the God we serve is able to deliver us from it,
and He will deliver us from Your Majesty's hand.
—*Daniel* 3:17

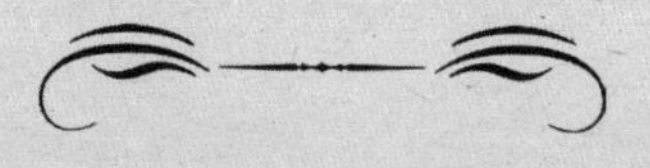

To Michael. Thanks for having my back.

ONE

Rebecca Miles dug her toes into the narrow crags of the Northern Ontario rock face, braced her legs against the granite and raised the lens of her video camera up to where jagged rock brushed against sky. Wind tugged her dark, shoulder-length hair free from its ponytail and sent it flying around her face. Something rustled in the trees far below her, but the quiver on the back of her neck told her not to look down. It was probably just the wind. Maybe an animal. But she couldn't imagine there'd be another person around for miles. She grabbed hold of a stubborn pine growing out of the rock to her right and focused on searching for the falcon's nest.

The climb up the embankment had turned out to be a whole lot steeper than she'd expected when she'd been standing safely on the ground, watching a pair of peregrines soar above. The narrow road got so little traffic, she could come and go for days without seeing another vehicle. It cut straight through a hill not far from the tiny patch of land she'd inherited from her mother. She'd left her camper and truck there, and hiked over. Now about fifty feet of steeply slanted rock and trees lay between her and the road below.

Something rumbled in the distance. It sounded like approaching thunder, but judging by the endless blue above, it was more likely a vehicle of some sort. Hopefully it wouldn't frighten off the birds. Falcons mated for life and at this time of year a circling pair often meant a nest. Good clear footage of fluffy white babies would cover both gas for her truck and basic groceries for a month or more. If she actually managed to catch a falcon family portrait, she'd have a solid chunk to put toward her next overseas trip.

Lord, You know I have a list a mile long of charity projects I'm hoping to film. But until then, help me just be thankful for everything I've got.

Freedom. Independence.

The ability to go where she wanted, film what interested her and have adventures on her own terms.

As a teenager, her happiest moments had been when she'd managed to slip away from her claustrophobic home life, to wander aimlessly around the now decommissioned military base at Remi Lake, a few hours north from where she now stood. Her mother had spent the first several years of Rebecca's life anxiously waiting for word from Rebecca's father—an absent man whom Rebecca had never met and wasn't supposed to ask about. Then, at thirteen, her mother had suddenly married General Arthur Miles—a decorated and larger-than-life hero in Canada's small, tight-knit military community, who'd encouraged Rebecca to call him "the General" and never "Dad." They'd moved onto the base, where she'd found herself with a twelve-year-old stepbrother named Seth, who'd never missed an opportunity to tell his gangly, awkward stepsister just how little he thought of her. She'd moved out at eighteen and hadn't seen the General since her mother's funeral, two years later, from a prescription meds overdose. But distancing herself from Seth had been more challenging.

She hadn't seen him in person for years, but that hadn't stopped him from bugging her online. The final straw had been when she'd set up a social media account and Seth had filled it with sarcastic comments. She'd blocked him instantly, only to have the computer engineer hack his way right back in. So she'd deleted the whole thing. Now, she could easily go days without checking her email, catching up on the news or even seeing another person.

Life was just simpler off the grid.

Her feet shifted. Pebbles cascaded down the hill beneath her. She tightened her grip and focused on searching for the nest. She'd started thinking about a falcon family and here her brain had rambled right on down the rabbit hole to thoughts of her own family life. Then she saw it. Three speckled eggs were nestled on a thin stone ledge. Rebecca smiled. She could use the winch on the back of her truck to raise a camera up here and monitor the feed through the video equipment in her camper. Her camera lens rose to the sky as she followed the adult falcons' flight. In falcon pairings both the male and female hunted. Both the male and female soared.

Instead of leaving one of them huddled at home in the nest.

She let out a long breath. This was the problem with camping and filming up here: it was all too easy to get stuck in the past, as memories of life on the Remi Lake military base nipped at the edges of her mind.

Why couldn't she let go of those years? Five years on base was enough to convince her that no matter how much she was drawn to the strength and courage of a man in uniform, she'd never put herself through the pain her mother had lived by falling for one. But there'd only ever been one young man on base to really tug on Rebecca's heartstrings. *Zack Biggs.* Orphaned when both of his parents had died in combat, he'd been living at Remi Lake with his aunt and uncle, who'd also served. Zack had been sweet, sensitive and every bit as introverted as she was. The exact opposite of big personalities like the General and Seth. She'd been the only teenage girl in the base's mixed martial arts class and clumsy to boot. Zack'd been husky and very overweight, but determined to get into shape, and with secret dreams of one day joining the special forces. They'd stuck together, as sparring partners and outsiders in a class full of confident jocks, like Seth. Zack was the closest she'd ever come to both a best friend and a high school crush. Closest she'd ever come to a date, too. When she'd been the surprise winner of a trophy for top student in the class, Zack had asked her to the formal sports banquet. She'd said yes. But he'd stood her up, only to then show up outside the hall, hours later in the pouring rain, to tell her that he'd just enlisted.

And she'd realized just how close she'd come to being in love with a military man.

The sound of the engine grew louder. The camera's volume meter was jumping. Her microphone was picking up the sound. She stopped recording and spun the camera's gaze toward the road, using the zoom function like a pair of binoculars. It was a motorcycle. Very nice machine, too. Harley-Davidson, maybe? If her memory of the General's collection was accurate. The bigger question was what it was even doing up here on this road to nowhere. She was hardly expecting company. He leaned into a skid and she caught a glimpse of an emblem with a red circle and a gold crown on the side of the bike. Canadian military. Infantry to be specific. Someone in the area on leave? Someone who'd gotten lost looking for the remains of the Remi Lake base?

The microphone picked up more rustling beneath her and this time her gaze followed the noise. A man in blue jeans and a toque had stepped out of the tree line, carrying what looked like a black softball. He was tall, but scrawny. Like a coyote who hadn't eaten in days. He tucked the black ball in a crag in the rocks beneath her, then went back for another two balls. Then he pulled out what looked like the remains of a cell phone. Her heart stopped as things she'd learned filming in war zones suddenly caught up to what her eyes were seeing now.

IEDs. *Improvised explosive devices.*

A terrorist's explosive weapon of choice.

And somebody was now planting them in the Ontario rock beneath her.

Questions shot rapid-fire through her mind, but she didn't give them time to form into words.

Thanks to the tree cover, the scrawny man might not even know she was standing on the rock above him. The man on the motorcycle probably had no idea the road was about to explode. All that mattered now was warning them both.

Adrenaline ran cold through her veins. The motorcycle rushed closer, the driver blind to the danger ahead. She prayed. *I'm the only hope he has, Lord. Please, show me what to do!* Her mind spun through the contents of her utility belt. She had a canister of bug spray, a small pocket knife, an air horn…

The motorcycle reached the final curve.

She grabbed the air horn and pressed. A deafening blare echoed through the rocks.

The motorcycle swerved sideways and for a moment she thought he'd managed to stop.

But it was too late.

An explosion filled the air, shaking the rock beneath her feet.

The bike flipped, crashing end over end.

She hugged the tree and braced her legs against the cliff.

The earth gave way beneath her feet.

Sergeant Zack Keats, recon specialist for the Canadian Forces' elite and highly classified counterterrorism force, hurtled through the air as the force of the explosion ripped the motorbike out from under him.

Hot smoke billowed around him, with the deafening roar of falling rocks. Just moments earlier he'd been cruising, feeling the wind beat against his body, wondering if he'd even find Rebecca Miles at her campsite. And if he did, how was he going to tell a woman he hadn't seen since the day she'd shattered his heart as a teenager that her stepbrother, Seth, was now a wanted criminal and traitor? Then he'd rounded a corner, a siren had sounded and the world had exploded around him.

A prayer for help moved through the soldier's mind as instinctively as his body adopted the position for impact.

Protect his neck. Curl his shoulders. Relax his body.

Save me, Lord. I need You now. But if this is it, have mercy—

The road hit him like a slab of concrete. Pain shot through his body. He bounced. His visor cracked. His bike was nothing but a tangled mass of metal to his right. Beyond it lay a pile of rubble from where rock and trees had slid down off the front of the cliff face, barricading the road ahead. At least most of the cliff was still standing.

Not the worst hit he'd ever taken. First as a soldier with Princess Patricia's Canadian Light Infantry, and then a part of the Canadian Forces joint task force for special ops, he'd spent most of his life in the world's roughest hot spots. Long before then, as a painfully sensitive and overweight young man, he'd taken his share of bullies' beatings, too, before he'd shed the last name he'd hated for a new one, converted his fat into muscle and refocused his emotional core into the kind of steady, unflappable determination needed to throw himself between the world's biggest bullies and those in need of rescue. But this ambush had definitely come without warning.

The world was still spinning. His ears were ringing. He ignored both, pressed a leather-gloved hand against the pavement and tensed himself to spring.

"Don't move." A lanky figure stepped out of the smoke. A ski mask covered his face and there was a handgun in his hand. A Glock. Almost certainly illegal.

Instinctively, Zack's hand reached for his own weapon, before remembering his firearm was unloaded and locked in his bag on the back of his bike, as was expected of him when on leave in Canada. Zack had always played by the rules. If it came to it, he'd die by them, too. But until that moment came, he was prepared to fight. His hand slid toward the knife in his ankle holster.

"I said, don't move." The masked man raised the gun. He sounded flustered and more than a little angry. "I don't want to shoot you, but I will if I have to."

Didn't want to shoot him? He'd just blown up the road. If the explosives had gone off just a few seconds later Zack would be dead now. So either this man was so desperate or foolish he didn't know what he was doing, or else he was lying through his teeth. But was he also Seth Miles, the traitor and criminal, that Zack was up here to talk to Rebecca about?

Zack fixed his gaze on the man's blue eyes, trying to mentally combine pictures from the news with his twenty-year-old memories of the bully who'd tormented him. Then he reminded himself that he still had no idea where the siren had come from.

"Look, I don't know who you are or what you want." Zack kept his hands steady and his voice calm. "But I don't want to fight you. Please, just let me search the area and make sure nobody else is in trouble."

The man hesitated. His eyes darted from what remained of the cliff side down to the rock pile now blocking the road. "There's nobody else here," he said. But his voice sounded far from confident.

"You sure about that? I heard an air horn. If you weren't the one who sounded it, then someone else did."

But this time, he ignored Zack's question. Instead, he stepped closer.

"You and I both know there's only one reason for anyone to be on this road." He pressed the barrel of his gun against the cracks in Zack's visor. "Get out of here. Don't come back. And stop looking for Seth Miles. He doesn't want to be found."

Zack would've snorted if the situation hadn't been deadly serious. Was he joking? This morning, Zack had been minding his own business, camping, quietly enjoying his last three days of home leave, when he'd hopped on his bike to go get gas and charge his cell phone. The coffee shop television had been blaring the news that authorities across North America had launched an all-out manhunt for Seth. Armed and presumed dangerous, according to the TV, Seth was wanted for treason, theft and attempted murder, after the computer engineer had abused his civilian military clearance, hacked into a government database, stolen something highly classified and then shot an unidentified woman in an Ottawa park.

But while news commentators and coffee-shop gossips had been hung up on how Seth was the only son of decorated hero General Arthur Miles, Zack's laser-sharp mind had suddenly filled with the adventurous eyes and wild dark hair of the only other person on earth who'd witnessed Seth's selfishness and bullying arrogance as Zack had. *Rebecca.* And the pledge Zack had made long ago, to always have her back. So he'd hopped on his bike and headed north, without even waiting for his phone to finish charging.

Seth wasn't his target. Apprehending Seth wasn't his mission. Still, he wasn't about to let a comment like that slide.

"Seth Miles is a coward and a traitor." Zack's voice rose. "He stole government secrets—"

Blue eyes flashed in fury. "He was protecting the country!"

"He shot an unarmed woman! Tried to murder her!"

"No! I didn't! I didn't shoot her!" Seth yelled. With a simple slip of the tongue he made his attempted disguise worthless.

Zack nearly chuckled through gritted teeth. "Oh, *you* didn't, did you, Seth? But you did steal sensitive information from your own country for a quick and easy payday?"

"You have no clue what I did or why I did it!" Seth flicked his handgun's safety switch off. "You stay away from me. You stay away from my sister. Or I'll kill you."

A muffled cry filled the air to Zack's right. Female. Frightened.

There was somebody trapped under those rocks and screaming for help. Seth's neck turned toward the sound. Zack kicked Seth's knees out and sent him sprawling. The Glock fired into the air. But Zack wrestled the weapon from Seth's grasp before he could fire again and leveled a swift blow to his jaw. Seth hit the pavement. His head snapped back. There was a chain around Seth's neck. A small blue computer memory stick hung from it. *The stolen government computer files?* Zack grabbed it and yanked it hard, breaking the chain from around Seth's neck. Then Zack ran for the rock pile. The voice had gone silent.

"Hello!" Zack scanned the rock pile. "Hey! Is somebody there?"

He tried to shove his visor up. It wouldn't budge. Then he heard it. A gasp. A cry. A voice, faint but strong, and coming from under the rocks. He saw fingers sliding out of a gap. A slender hand, clad in a climbing glove.

"I'm here. It's okay. I've got you." He climbed across the rocks, crouched down and touched her hand lightly, just enough to reassure her. Out of the corner of his eye he could see Seth scrambling to his feet.

Zack's brain went into triage mode. He had to stop Seth. He had to save the woman beneath the rocks. He couldn't let a traitor escape. He couldn't let a civilian die.

"Please, Lord," she gasped. "I don't want to die down here."

The woman's prayer yanked Zack's attention back to the rocks. Seth disappeared over the other side of the rubble. Zack grabbed a boulder, hoisted it up and threw it off the pile. Then he looked down. Dark, determined eyes looked up at him. Black hair lay dusty and wild around a sun-kissed face. Her delicate lips parted but no sound came out. Zack's heart beat painfully in his chest, with the same unexpected sting he'd felt as a teenager, as he looked across the gym martial arts mats and suddenly laid eyes on the most beautiful person he'd ever seen.

It was Rebecca.

TWO

Rebecca nearly cried out in frustration as a black shape suddenly blocked out the tiny patch of blue sky that had appeared over her head. It took her two deep breaths to realize she was staring straight into the helmet visor of the man from the motorcycle. He must've realized it, too, because he said, "Hey, sorry," and reached to yank the helmet off.

Another gunshot split the air. He muttered something about a second gun and disappeared from view.

She closed her eyes and tried not to panic. *Thank You, God, that I'm still alive and nothing seems to be broken.* When she'd seen smoke from the explosion rushing up toward her, and felt the rock slide out from under her feet, she'd held tight with everything she had, until there was no ground left beneath her and nothing to do but fall. Then she'd protected her head with her arms and focused on controlling her slide the best she could as the world around her was swallowed up in smoke, heat and falling rock.

More shouting from above her now. A gun blast rattled the rocks. She closed her eyes and focused on breathing through her fear, even as she could feel it threatening to take over her mind. A vehicle engine rumbled in the distance. There was the sound of someone scrambling over the rocks above her again.

"Hey." The voice was male, deep and with just a hint of grit. "I'm back. You okay?"

Rebecca opened her eyes.

Her heart stopped. His helmet was now off. And she found herself staring straight into the gray eyes of the only man who'd ever managed to make that heart flutter a beat.

Zack. She opened her mouth but couldn't find her voice. *Zack Biggs.*

Is that really you?

"Hang on, I'm going to get you out of here." He disappeared again and she heard rocks shift above her.

No, he couldn't be Zack. She must've bumped her head so hard she was seeing things. Her mind filled with a mental image of what Zack had looked like the last time she'd seen him. She'd been seventeen years old and dressed in the only sparkling formal dress she'd ever owned. The sports banquet had been over. She'd still been clutching her martial arts trophy: *Rebecca Miles, Technically Flawless.* Zack had stood outside in the courtyard, pounding rain beating on his head and running down his face. Looking sad and angry and as though he'd just lost something.

The weight that was pressing against her limbs lightened. She wriggled her other arm out of the rock.

"All right, I'm going to reach in and lift you out of there." He peeled off his leather jacket and leaned in toward her. "Just grab hold of my arms, and I'll hoist you up."

The arms she grabbed ahold of were solid muscle and as smooth as marble encased in silk. The T-shirt-clad chest that pulled her in was as perfectly sculpted as a statue. The face she looked into had cheekbones cut like an action hero's, and his black hair was grizzled gray at the temples. Could this man really be Zack? If so, didn't he recognize her? Her tongue felt tied. His strong arms were practically carrying her down to the road, and here her brain couldn't even figure out how to make sense of what was happening. A good chunk of the cliff side now blocked the road leading to her campsite. The man who'd set the detonators was nowhere to be seen. The motorbike lay in a twisted wreck on the south side of the rocks. The Zack she'd known had had a passion for motorcycles and had admired the General's vintage collection. But he also could never have maneuvered a bike like that. He set her down gently. One hand hovered over her shoulder. "Are you hurt?"

"Scratched and bruised, but okay," she said. "But what about you? That looked like a pretty major crash."

"I'm fine." He stepped back. His shoulders straightened. His arms crossed. Everything about his stance screamed military.

"Where did that other man go?" she asked. "Do you know who he was, or where he went, or why he sabotaged the road like that?" She was talking too fast, which tended to happen when she was uncomfortable. And right now her nerves were in overdrive. "I don't have a cell phone on me, but there's one in my camper, which is a short walk from here. My truck's there, too. We need to report this to police. This road's a write-off, at least for going south. And your bike's wrecked. But if we take my truck and drive north, there's a back way we can take to Timmins. It'll only take a couple hours."

He just looked at her. Then he ran one hand slowly over his face and looked down the road.

See, this is why you can't possibly be my Zack, no matter how much you remind me of him. Because my Zack would be hugging me right now and reassuring me, instead of just standing there.

"Sorry, we haven't done introductions." She stepped forward and stretched out her hand. "My name is Rebecca Miles."

His eyes met her gaze. She knew those eyes. Dark gray. Like flint, the moment just before it sparked a fire. His mouth opened. A phone started ringing behind her, so loudly she almost jumped. He ran past her, back up the rock pile to his jacket, and grabbed a cell phone out of the pocket. "Keats here."

Keats? His name was Keats? Even though she'd just told herself he couldn't possibly be her high school crush, somehow hearing a different name come out of the man's mouth landed heavy in her stomach.

She watched as he stood on the rock, his back to her and his phone to his ear. If he'd had a phone, why hadn't he called the police already? The conversation was quick. He hung up, picked up his jacket and walked back down the rock slide toward her. Deep frown lines cut along his brow.

"Keats, is it?" she asked.

He paused, as though he'd just been asked a very difficult question.

"I'm sorry," she added. "I couldn't help but hear when you answered the phone. But that's all I heard."

"Yes." He pulled off his right glove and reached for her hand. A strong, firm grasp enveloped hers. "Sergeant Keats. Reconnaissance specialist. That was my CO—my commanding officer—on the phone. I apprised him of the situation. My phone battery is pretty much dead right now, and he's going to call all this in to the police. And yes, I'd like to take you up on your offer of a ride to Timmins." There was a searching look on his face, as if she was supposed to be reading something else between his words. "What were you doing up on that hill?"

"Searching for a falcon's nest," she said. "I'm a filmmaker and videographer. So, Sergeant Keats, is it safe to presume that the man who nearly blew us up is some target you're up here chasing?"

"No." His frown grew deeper. "I'm not on assignment. I'm on leave actually, until Thursday. I'm due back at base in two days. Just let me grab my bag off the bike and I'll be good to go."

"But what about the man who blew up the road? I heard arguing and gunshots—"

"He's gone."

Her hands slid onto her hips. "And?"

"And, he blew up the road." Now his arms crossed over his chest. "We struggled. I disarmed him. He ran off to where he'd hidden his vehicle. I thought he'd gone. But then he returned with a new weapon. It discharged. I disarmed him again. He left. I now have two illegal Glocks in my possession, and I'd like to go put them in my bag, as I don't much feel like leaving them here."

It was all useful information, but hardly warm and reassuring. And didn't tell her what she wanted to know.

"But *who* was he and why did he blow up the road?"

"I'm really sorry, but I'm afraid I can't tell you anything more than I have." He turned around and climbed back over the rocks toward his motorcycle.

"But are we still in danger from him?"

He paused, his feet balancing on the crushing rocks that she'd feared just moments ago would bury her alive. His eyes glanced at the sky, his head shook and his lips moved as though he was praying. Then he looked at her head-on, with a look so raw and unflinching she blinked. "I don't honestly know if we're in danger or not. But trust me, Rebecca, I'll do everything in my power to keep you safe. And I wish I could tell you more about what's going on. I really do."

He grabbed a green shoulder bag and moved his bike off the road. They walked to her camper. Neither of them spoke. He'd already made it clear he wasn't about to answer any of her questions, and random small talk had never been something she'd been good at. Eventually they reached the small break in the trees that was the unpaved, overgrown entrance to her property. It was a nice chunk of forest actually. But it was hard to reach and very overgrown. Terrible for building on. But not bad for a hideaway.

"Welcome to my home." She waved a hand toward the vintage aluminum camper now hitched to the back of a large black pickup truck. It was the same camper she'd lived in before her mom married the General, one of the few things she'd inherited. "Not much to look at, but it has all my video equipment inside. I travel a lot, so all I really need is a place to park my life when I'm not on the road. Feel free to dump your stuff in the front seat."

"Thank you. Can I charge my phone in your

truck? My battery's almost dead, and I promised my CO I'd call him back."

"No problem." She tossed him her keys. He caught them smoothly. "My minilaptop computer is plugged in there, but you can just stick it in the glove compartment. I've also got a portable generator running in the camper, if you'd rather."

"Thanks. I think I'll go with the truck. It'll get us on the road faster." He slid one hand into the front pocket of his jeans as if checking to make sure something was there. "Hey, this might sound like an odd request, but would it be okay if I checked something on your laptop?"

She shrugged. "Be my guest. But it's really small and it won't connect to the internet."

Rebecca walked to her camper. For a moment she debated simply unhitching her truck and leaving the camper in the woods. But depending on how long things took at the police station, she might just as well spend the night at a campsite in Timmins. Small and portable, with four wheels, it might not be everyone's idea of home. But for her, it was perfect. A narrow single bunk lay at the front end of the camper. A tiny kitchenette with a fold-down table filled the center of the space. At the back end, the second bunk had been converted into a long, makeshift desk and video-editing space.

Her eyes rose to the computer monitors at the end of the camper. She'd left them running on the generator. One was broadcasting a feed from the tiny camera mounted inside of her truck. Clipped just inside of the sun visor, she used the tiny, temperamental spy camera to film either herself or the road ahead when her project called for her to narrate something while driving. Right now, it showed the mysterious Sergeant Keats. He plugged a memory stick into her laptop computer. Then he opened his bag on the seat beside him. She crossed the camper to turn off the feed. His phone rang again. He answered.

"Hello?" he said. "Yeah. Sorry we got cut off. Yeah, I'm with her. No, I haven't told her anything. I'm pretty sure she doesn't have a clue."

A shiver ran down her spine. She shouldn't be eavesdropping. But he was talking about her and keeping something from her. Why should she trust him?

"Yeah, I've got it. I'm using her laptop to check the contents now. But it seems to be automatically downloading onto her machine." He stuck the phone between his ear and his shoulder, picked up her laptop. "I don't know. Something weird's going on. I'll call back when I've got something to report. But yeah, I've got Rebecca." He set the laptop back down. "Don't worry. I know what I need to do here! I'm not about to let anything get in the way of doing it. Fair enough? I'll find out what she knows, if she knows anything, and I'll bring her in."

She froze.

He was talking like she was his target. No, it was worse than that. She was a Canadian citizen standing on home soil. He wasn't the police. He didn't have a warrant or any legal right to question her or take her anywhere. But he was talking as if she was his prisoner.

"No, Rebecca doesn't know anything!" Zack seemed to be searching his bag for something. His voice sounded almost exasperated. "She's completely clueless. She's completely in the dark. She doesn't even know who I am."

He reached for the sun visor and tilted the rearview mirror to look behind him, bumping the tiny camera. The camera's view shifted to the side of the passenger seat. The audio feed cut out entirely. She could barely see a thing inside the cab now and couldn't hear another word he said.

He waved his hand through the camera's

gaze and suddenly she could see what he'd been searching for.

Her hand rose to her lips.

It was a pair of handcuffs.

Zack tucked the handcuffs into his belt and his SIG semiautomatic into his holster. Next time he ran into Seth, he'd be ready for him. The two Glocks he'd taken off Seth now lay disassembled in the bottom of his bag. He did not want to know what kind of friends Seth had been making that he managed to get ahold of not only two illegal handguns, but also an IED. Hopefully, he was just a really good thief.

Either way, frustration coursed through Zack's shoulders. Stonewalling Rebecca like that had been almost physically painful. But she hadn't seemed to recognize him. He'd been trying to figure out what to say when Seth had opened fire again. He'd sorted that, and then his phone had rung with a call from his own CO, Major Jeff Lyons, field commander of Zack's special ops unit. And Jeff had opened with the line, *Please tell me you're nowhere near Rebecca Miles right now.*

Zack blew out a hard breath. Yes, it was no secret that he had an old Remi base newspaper clipping inside his footlocker with a picture of Rebecca at seventeen and a story about how she'd won the martial arts trophy. Or that he sometimes got a bit of good-natured ribbing from the other guys about having a crush on General Arthur Miles's stepdaughter whenever the General's face was on TV. Even though he'd never personally met the man, even back when he and Rebecca were teenagers.

But he'd never imagined that as news of Seth Miles's treason and crimes spread like wildfire through both official and unofficial channels, someone in his unit would suddenly hope that Zack hadn't gone to try to talk to Seth's sister. Or that his own CO would then give him a friendly call just to suggest that as Rebecca was now wanted for police questioning, it might be a good idea that Zack stay away from her.

Too late for that.

"Again, I can't assess what was on the memory stick." Zack looked at the laptop. "Whatever it was, it appears to have now leaped from the memory stick to the laptop, and scrubbed the memory stick clean of any trace on the way out. Now the laptop's completely locked down and appears to be asking for a password in Cyrillic script. So one of the Slavic languages. Don't think it's Russian. Could be either another Eastern European or a North Asian language."

He could think of at least four different organized crime groups his task force had tangled with in various parts of the world that used Cyrillic script in their communications. He'd personally gone into Eastern Europe a few months ago to safely extract a brilliant young woman from the clutches of one such group. *And I really hope whatever this is, it's not connected to that.* Because the idea that Seth Miles could've just hacked around the government database, looking for something to steal, and found something significant to an active special forces operation was unthinkable.

"Bring it in. Bring Rebecca Miles in. Walk away," Jeff said. "I'll report up the chain of command how fortunate we are that one of our top recon guys just happened to stumble upon Seth Miles's current location and might've retrieved what he stole. I'll try to play it as such great news that hopefully it won't come back and bite you."

"I'm on leave," Zack said. "It was a personal errand. I simply saw her face on the news, and decided to pop by and see how she was. I was hardly expecting to run into Seth."

"Oh, I know. You don't need to convince me of anything," the major said. "This isn't an order and we're not officially having this conversation. But as your friend, Zack, my advice is to get as far away from this mess as possible. And fast. The last thing we want is for our whole unit to be grounded from deployment because one of our top guys is being questioned in connection to an open treason investigation. The RCMP are heading the investigation, in conjunction with the Canadian Department of National Defence, and we haven't been called in. But I can tell you that once word got out a member of our unit had a personal relationship with Seth Miles's sister, it raised some serious flags as to where the break in security could've come from. We're already worried that we can't seem to stem the leak of Canadian equipment ending up in the hands of Slavic organized crime. If someone from the RCMP sits down to interview Miss Miles and she so much as mentions your name it won't look good. Not for you. Not for us. As a friend, I would hate to see this unit function without you. But you know we can't afford to be pulled from deployment because there's a shadow hanging over one guy."

Okay, okay. He got all that. Even though he didn't like it. Maybe coming to check in on Rebecca had been the wrong call. It had been twenty years since Zack'd let his heart have any say in his decision making, and it had probably been a mistake to start now. But still…

"The Rebecca I knew was a reasonable person with a good heart," he said. "I know you've advised me to keep her in the dark, and I understand why. But I'm not convinced it'll jeopardize the investigation by telling her who I am and why I'm here. Honestly, she'll go squirrelly if I'm not straight with her."

Rebecca's tenacity could be pretty unrelenting. Considering how hard she'd hammered him for information on the road, he could just imagine how the truck ride to Timmins would go.

"When in doubt," Jeff said, "imagine explaining every single call you make in the next hour, in a long, drawn-out, extremely uncomfortable tribunal on this whole Seth Miles mess, and answering the question why a soldier who's withstood intense questioning by foreign militants couldn't withstand the badgering of a cute girl with pretty eyes."

Zack snorted. "She's more than cute. But point taken. We'll be in Timmins in a little over an hour."

Then, sometime after his next deployment, he'd write her a nice long letter, apologizing for not being straight with her, not to mention infecting her laptop with some kind of Slavic virus. Hopefully, she'd forgive him.

"And you're convinced she's not complicit in her brother's crimes?" Jeff asked.

"One hundred percent."

"Okay. I hope for your sake you're right. Just don't let Rebecca or that laptop out of your sight. If you see Seth, don't engage unless you have no other option. Again, I can't authorize you for a mission, because it's not *our* investigation, and I can't dictate what you do with your personal leave. As your friend, feel free to call me anytime. But if this escalates, I'm going to have to get involved as your commanding officer. Got it?"

"Got it." Zack ran one hand over the back of his neck. "I'm sorry for giving you an extra headache and I won't do anything that brings the unit into disrepute."

"You're the only man I know who could go on leave, to the middle of nowhere in Northern Ontario, and land in the middle of a major international crisis."

"Ha, ha," Zack said. "Thanks for calling. I mean it."

"Anytime. See you back at base."

The call ended. He put the laptop back into its hard case, zipped it up and then slid it into the truck's glove compartment, happy to see she'd had the smarts to install a combination lock on it. He shoved his bag deep under the passenger seat and then got out of the truck. The door to Rebecca's camper was closed. He strode toward it.

He had to admit, he kind of hated how all this was unfolding. If only Rebecca had recognized him. But a woman like her had probably been approached by so many male suitors in the past twenty years that one shy guy from when she was a teenager would have been long forgotten.

Lord, help me handle this situation honorably, honestly and with a whole lot of wisdom.

He wouldn't disclose what he couldn't disclose. But he also wouldn't lie. And if that led to being barraged by questions for the whole truck ride to Timmins, so be it. He knocked on the door.

"Hey, Rebecca, you about ready to go?"

No answer. He silently counted to three and then opened the door. The camper was empty. He stepped inside. A window behind the sink was open. He nearly groaned. *You've got to be kidding me!* Oh, he'd had more than a few targets try to escape his grasp during his career. A few had even managed to land a blow or two before getting restrained. But none had ever made it as far as the threshold, let alone stepping one foot out the door.

And here Rebecca had actually evaded him by climbing out a window?

Something cold and metal brushed the back of his neck.

"Don't move," Rebecca said. "And get your hands up."

And now he would've been tempted to laugh if the situation wasn't so serious. His hands rose, just enough to show that he'd heard her. Surely she'd know how easily someone with his training could disarm her. The only reason for him to even hesitate was to minimize the risk of *her* getting hurt. Not to mention that if they got into a physical altercation he'd probably have to report it, and that would hardly help her case when it came to proving her innocence in Seth's crimes. "Rebecca, look, I don't know what you think you're doing, but I'm not about to hurt you."

What was she even holding? Definitely metal, but not sharp enough of an edge to be a knife. Cylindrical, but it didn't feel like the barrel of a gun, either.

"I want to believe you." Her body brushed up against his back. Her breath tickled his ear. The scent of her hair filled his lungs. "But you haven't exactly been honest with me, Sergeant."

"Okay, you're right, I didn't answer all of your questions earlier. I'm sorry, there are just some things I can't tell you." He spun around, grabbed both her wrists in one swift motion and held her hands above their heads. "Now, drop your weapon."

Rebecca was pinned against his chest, so close that if he'd just leaned forward a couple of inches he could've kissed her nose. She'd donned a simple gray windbreaker since he'd seen her last. The hood was pulled up over her head and closed tight, leaving a few black wisps of hair framing her face. Rebecca buried her face deep inside his chest. Something clicked above him. He glanced up. There was a small, metal canister of high-potency bug spray in her hands. She fired, using his chest to shield her own face. Bug spray filled the air above them, burning his eyes and choking his throat. Her wrists slipped from his grasp. Then she bolted out of the camper, through the trees.

Wow. Somebody had apparently kept her skills since they'd last sparred. Not to mention adding a new skill or two. He'd never been sprayed like a bug before. He chased after her. His eyes watered. His vision blurred. "Rebecca, wait! I'm—" A fit of coughing stole the words from this throat.

Lord, help me figure out how to stop Rebecca and calm her down before someone gets hurt.

He ran after her. She didn't even try to double back to her truck. Instead, she cut straight through the trees, as though she was trying to reach the main road. She was faster than he remembered. She'd always been lithe. But the years had added strength to her limbs.

"Rebecca! Stop!" Surely she had to know there was no point running. He was going to catch up with her. She burst out of the trees and started down the road. Then he heard a vehicle.

Oh no. No, no, no... Why is there another vehicle on this road?

"Help!" Her voice echoed through the trees. "Help! Stop!"

Tires screeched. Zack pushed his legs faster. But it was too late. A red moving van had reached the rock barrier and seemed to be turning around. Smiling stick-figure animals on the side advertised Woodland Home Movers.

"Rebecca! Wait!"

She reached the van. The back door opened. He couldn't let her leap into a random van, no matter the cost.

He stopped chasing her, stood on the road and gasped a breath.

"Becs!" he shouted. "It's me! Zack! Zack Biggs!"

She turned back. The hood slipped from her head. Hair fell loose around her face. "*Zack?* It's actually you."

"Yeah." He risked taking a step toward her, as though she was a nervous animal he didn't want to spook. *Just please don't get in that van.* "My name is Zack Keats now. New name. New look. But yeah, it's still me."

"I thought...I mean, I kind of knew..." Her dark eyes opened wide like a camera lens struggling to bring a picture into focus. "Why didn't you just tell me?"

"Well, if you knew, why didn't you just ask?" He reached his hand out toward her. "I'm sorry, forgive me. I had my reasons. Please don't go with them."

"Look, Zack, I—"

A scream stole the words from her lips as a burly, tattooed man reached out from the back door and yanked her backward into the van.

"Rebecca!" Zack pelted toward the van. For a second he could still see her legs kicking and prayed she'd break free. Then the van door slammed, trapping Rebecca inside.

A second heavily tattooed man leaned out

of the driver's window and fired a semiautomatic. Bullets flew past Zack's head. Rebecca's screams filled the air.

But neither shook Zack anywhere near as much as the two-headed black-and-red bird-of-prey tattoo on the driver's bulging arm.

These men were members of Black Talon, a highly dangerous Eastern European organized crime syndicate.

And they'd just kidnapped Rebecca.

THREE

The hollow sound of the door slamming echoed in Rebecca's ears. The van was picking up speed. The burly bearded thug who'd manhandled her into the vehicle pressed a gun to her temple. But it was the huge hand holding tight to her throat that filled her with such blinding pain that for a moment she couldn't begin to find a way to fight back. He shoved her down into the cold empty back of the moving van and pinned her to the floor.

Help me, Lord. I need to escape this van before it gets to wherever they're taking me.

She looked around. Inside the vehicle she could see two guns, two kidnappers, but nothing within her reach that she could grab as a weapon. Outside the vehicle was the muscular bulk and courage of the one guy she would've trusted with her life. Would he rescue her now?

She looked up at the man now holding her down. There was a crude, vaguely Eastern European tattoo on his neck, of two red-and-black eagles that almost seemed to be crawling out from under his shirt, and the word *Ivan.*

He yelled something to the driver, but it wasn't in English. Then the van lurched forward. "Ivan" let go of her body but kept his weapon aimed at her face.

"You down! No move!" The order came from the driver. The same bird-of-prey tattoo was on his arm, this one with *Dmitry.*

Were those their first names? A family name? Or some other distinction?

Dmitry was trying to drive forward with one hand and shoot backward out the window at Zack with the other. He shouted something at Ivan in a language Rebecca couldn't understand.

Ivan shouted back in heavily accented English. "She's down! She's not going to move!"

Oh, how little those men knew her.

The sound of a bullet cracked the air outside the van. Zack was returning fire. Then the back window shattered in a spray of class. She sprung to her hands and feet in a racing stance, prayer crossing her mind even as glass rained down around them. Ivan swore. The van swerved. Rebecca glanced back through the open gap in the shattered glass and saw Zack running after her, gun in hand.

His body strong. His face fierce.

I still don't know what's going on. But, old sparring partner, I'm glad you've got my back.

Zack was getting smaller and smaller in the distance, though, as the van kept driving. Ivan fired through the broken window, the explosion filling the metal vehicle like an echo chamber. Dmitry turned back and screamed at Ivan. But it was all the distraction she needed.

Rebecca leaped to her feet and charged. She grabbed the driver from behind and pressed her fingers into his eyes. Dmitry swore. The van spun wildly. Forcing the van to crash would be dangerous. But the van still hadn't picked up that much speed, and something told her she was far safer in a collision with Zack running to her rescue than she would be going wherever these men were taking her. Ivan grabbed her hair. Dmitry stomped on the breaks. The van slammed to a stop, throwing Rebecca against the seat and tossing Ivan across the floor. Rebecca recovered first. She ran for the van's back door, her feet crunching on broken glass. She could hear her abductors shouting behind her. She grabbed the door handle. The door flew open, wrenching the handle from her hand.

It was Zack. She nearly fell out of the van into his arms. Zack's free hand grabbed her waist, just long enough to help her onto the ground. But then, before letting go, he whispered in her ear, "I need you to trust me and do whatever I say, without question."

"What?"

But Zack stepped back. His head tilted in her direction. "You! Get down! Now!"

Zack was shouting *at her.* Not at the men who'd just abducted her. She hesitated. Her feet weren't two steps away from the kidnappers' van. Thick, endless forest spread out around her on every side. And Zack just expected her to drop to the ground instead of running?

Dmitry climbed out the driver's-side door. Ivan stumbled across the back of the van toward them. Zack's eyes cut sideways at Rebecca.

"Do it!" Zack said. "Trust me! Just get down."

Her head shook. "But—"

Ivan's bulk filled the van's back door. With one large, steady hand he aimed his gun at Zack's face and barked something in a foreign language. Zack didn't move a muscle. Dmitry walked around the side of the van, slowly.

"She's coming with us." Dmitry trained his gun on Zack's face.

Zack paused a long moment, without moving or speaking, as if he didn't even see the guns or the men behind them. Then Zack shrugged and shook his head.

"She? You mean, this one?" Zack pointed one finger at Rebecca, shook his head and tapped his chest in a slow, exaggerated motion. "No, no. She's coming with me."

Ivan laughed. It was an ugly sound bordering on a snarl. His finger hovered on the trigger. "No, I kill you. She comes with me."

Rebecca stood, with broken glass under her boots and legs tensed to spring. Zack was so calm and so in control, it was as if he was haggling over the price of meat instead of fighting for her life. Something within her tugged at the corner of her heart, reminding her of the sweet, sensitive man who she'd once trusted enough to spar with. She'd trusted Zack with her life back then. He was the first man she'd ever really trusted.

But how could she trust him now?

He'd kept secrets from her. He hadn't told her who he was. Her life was in danger and he was being so casual about it, he was almost cold. Zack hadn't just transformed his body to look like the jocks who'd once made them both feel worthless. Now he sounded just like them, too.

Zack shrugged again, rolling his shoulders up and down in a slow rise and fall that seemed to accentuate every curve of his muscular chest.

"This one, she's a bit difficult. Clumsy, you know, and a chatterbox." He made a mouth with his fingers and flapped it up and down in the same dismissive "talking" gesture Seth had once used to hurt and belittle her. "But I promised my boss I'd take her somewhere. You understand how this works. You have a job to do. I have a job to do. Maybe we can figure something out. How much is your boss paying you for her?"

The question hung in the air. Ivan and Dmitry glanced at each other. Neither answered. And now, Rebecca was too angry to even let the fear she was feeling even take hold. Zack didn't look at her. One of Zack's hands still held the gun firmly in its grip. The other was just inches away from it. She used to feel so safe in his arms. She didn't doubt either the speed or aim he'd be able to pull the trigger with. But now, standing next to him, she felt anything but safe. She felt like that awkward, clumsy female in the martial arts class nobody wanted to get stuck with.

No, worse than that. She felt like a worthless scrap of meat in a dogfight.

"Ivan, is it?" Zack nodded to the man's tattoo on the man's neck. His voice rose. "You don't want to take this woman. She's a bad assignment. Cut your losses and move on. It's not worth the trouble."

Ivan snapped something at Dmitry. Dmitry shouted back. In an instant, both men were arguing so loudly they were almost bellowing.

Zack tilted his head and leaned toward Rebecca. "Trust me, okay? Do whatever I say to do. Without question."

"No bribe!" Ivan shouted in English. "No money. No deal. No bribe. We're taking her now." He pointed one finger at Rebecca. "You. Girlie. Hands up. Come here, now."

She nearly laughed. Did these men not see the gun Zack had trained at their heads? True, it was two guns against one, but it was not as if Zack was about to let them drive off with her.

"Okay, okay." Zack lowered his gun and forced an artificial chuckle from this throat.

What? she nearly screamed inside her own head.

Ivan's snarl turned into a smirk. "You're just going to give us the girl?"

Zack shrugged. "What can I say? Like I said, she is clumsy. She will take two steps, trip over her own feet and fall down."

Ivan snapped something to Dmitry.

"No, no, don't shoot me, Dmitry!" Zack

raised his hands. "You shoot me. I shoot you. Ivan here gets the girl and the money."

There was a long pause. Wind brushed the trees. Ivan shifted his feet. Zack stood firm on the pavement.

Zack turned to Rebecca. "Go around to the passenger's-side door. I'll stay here with this man and we'll work things out."

Her head shook. Tears were forming in her eyes. "If I get into their van, they'll kill me."

Firm gray eyes cut at Rebecca. "Passenger side. Go."

Zack could feel his heart beating in his chest, slow and steady.

He could sense Rebecca beside him without even looking her way. He knew how she was standing and how her limbs were moving. He knew exactly how much space was between their two bodies. He could feel the fear rolling off her shoulders like waves. He could hear the ragged, desperate sound of her breathing and wished there was a way he could still it.

Trust me, Becs. Please. I know what I'm doing. I know who these men are, how they think and how to keep you safe. Just walk around to the passenger side of the van, take two steps and hit the ground.

What were two members of Black Talon,

a violent Eastern European crime syndicate, even doing in Canada? There'd been rumors recently of an internal power struggle within Black Talon. Members killing other members for control of the syndicate. What was more worrying was that both Canadian intelligence and weapons kept turning up in the hands of one faction. His special ops unit had recently been tasked with trying to determine, without any real leads, where the leak was coming from. It was possible these two men were former members who'd gotten ahold of forged immigration documents from the same source, come to North America and turned mercenaries for hire. But the hackles on the back of his neck, and the way they'd responded to his questions about their boss, made him suspect they were the real deal.

Did they suspect he was Canadian military? He'd tried to throw them off by calling them "Dmitry" and "Ivan" as if he thought the tattoos were the men's real names, as opposed to the names of their first confirmed kills.

All Zack was waiting for now was for Rebecca to get herself out of harm's way. Then he could rush Ivan and safely disarm him. After that he'd take out Dmitry.

But Rebecca wasn't moving. Had she not understood his signal? Did his directions confuse her? True, they hadn't seen each other in years. But they used to be so tight it was as though they could read each other's thoughts. The soldier in Zack told him that when the hostage one was rescuing became a liability, it was important to focus on the key mission objective above all else.

Yet something in his heart was stopping him from thinking of Rebecca as a mere "hostage" or "objective." Rebecca was different. Somehow. Keeping her safe mattered to him. But he didn't have time to stand around asking himself how or why. If she didn't move soon, he'd have no choice but to treat her like any other uncooperative hostage he was trying to rescue, which was something he really didn't want to have to do.

Aw, come on, Rebecca! Until you move I won't be able to get us out of this!

Zack tilted his head toward Rebecca but kept his eyes trained on the gunmen.

"Hurry up," he hissed.

Ivan raised an eyebrow.

Lord, he prayed, *help her understand. I can't keep stalling these men forever.*

"Look, please, don't make this any harder than it needs to be," Zack said, sharply. "You think I don't remember how *clumsy* you were? Like I said, you'd take two steps onto the martial arts mats, trip and you would wipe out on your face. Just go around to the side of the van and get out of my way. Now! You don't want them to tie you up or drag you off kicking and screaming, now do ya?"

Rebecca spun on her heels—

Thank You, God!

She sprinted hard into the woods.

No!

Ivan swore and fired after her. Dmitry charged into the trees.

No. No. No. No. No.

This is exactly the kind of situation Zack had wanted to avoid! Rebecca was now running off wildly with no direction or focus with an experienced killer on her heels, putting her own life in even worse danger. Why hadn't she just listened?

Ivan's weapon swung toward Zack. But Zack wasn't about to let him get off another shot. Zack charged, head down, his full strength barreling into the thug like a freight train. Ivan's body smacked against the pavement. The gun flew from his hand.

Zack stood over him and grabbed him by the shirt collar. "Why is the Black Talon in Canada? How did you get into the country? Who's been supplying you with Canadian weapons? What do you want with Rebecca Miles?"

"No English." The criminal spat in his face.

A gun blast sounded from the trees to his left.

Rebecca.

Dmitry was still hunting her.

Zack's jaw clenched. If he let Ivan get away he might never get an answer. But if he didn't, Rebecca might die. He leveled one decisive blow at the side Ivan's head, hard enough to keep him from following. Then Zack grabbed the man's gun and charged into the woods. His feet pelted quickly through the trees. His ears strained for noise to guide him.

Zack had always been a tracker. Before he'd been a soldier he'd hunted game, both large and small, in the Canadian woods. As a bodyguard one summer, he'd found and returned the runaway rich kid he'd been hired to protect. But while his body moved almost silently, his heart pounded so loudly in his ears, it threatened to block out the world around him. Rebecca hadn't taken him seriously. She hadn't respected him. She hadn't seen the man he'd become. *A man finally worthy of being respected and cared for by a woman like her.* She must still think of him as the emotionally and physically weak boy he used to be. And now her life was in danger because of it.

Another gun blast.

Then Dmitry's voice, loud and angry. "Come out now!"

Zack crept toward the sound. He could see Dmitry between the trees. The criminal was standing in a clearing. But where was Rebecca? Dmitry swung his weapon around in a circle and fired wildly into the underbrush. Bullets tore through the trees.

"You! Out! Now!" Dmitry's gun spun wildly from one direction to another. "Or I'll hurt you!"

Zack held in his breath as bullets flew past him, exploding in the underbrush. Dmitry reached to reload.

Rebecca leaped from the trees.

FOUR

Zack watched in amazement as Rebecca launched herself at Dmitry, landing hard on the criminal's back. The gun flew from Dmitry's hand and disappeared into the undergrowth. Rebecca clung to his back, swinging at his head and scratching like a wildcat. So, she'd been hiding up a tree waiting for a member of Black Talon to run out of bullets? Rebecca might not be the easiest target he'd ever extracted from danger, but the woman had serious guts.

Zack burst through the tree line and started running. Dmitry tossed Rebecca to the ground. She leaped up and charged right back at the burly man, even as his fist flew at her. She fell back. But only for a moment. She charged again.

"Rebecca, wait!" Zack threw the strength of his bulk in between Rebecca and the professional killer. Dmitry swung toward Zack.

Zack blocked the blow and leveled a decisive punch at the man's jaw. Rebecca took off running through the woods again.

You've got to be kidding me!

The Black Talon killer scrambled to his feet and took off running back toward the road. Rebecca and Dmitry had disappeared through the trees in opposite directions.

Okay, now what? Zack glanced up to the sky, but even before a prayer could leave his lips, he knew exactly which way to run.

Zack took off after Rebecca. He gave up on stealth and went for speed. She was smaller, lither and better able to weave through the dense underbrush. He felt like a rhinoceros crashing after her. But she would never be able to beat the sheer strength of the adrenaline that surged in his veins. He caught up to her, slowly and surely. Then for a moment they were pacing each other, his feet just a few steps behind hers.

Zack's hand reached out and brushed her shoulder, even as he dreaded the moment he was going to have to grab her and force her to stop. "Rebecca." He panted. "Please."

She stopped running. So did he. They stood there together, face-to-face in the forest, catching their breath. Her hands grabbed both of her knees, as her head swung down between her legs for a moment, panting. Then she swung her head back up, and he watched as dark hair cascaded around her shoulders, dancing like grass in the wind. His mouth went dry.

Rebecca's hands rose up in front of her face in two small fists. He watched as her legs moved into the perfect lines of a fighter's stance. Something inside his stomach lurched. He watched her take the pose he'd seen her take so many times before, back on the mats when they were so much younger and knew each other so much better. His heart remembered how there'd always been a slight smile on her lips and a twinkle in her eyes as she challenged him to a fight. Now, the look in her eyes was deadly serious and the curl of her lip almost trembled.

His heart sank down to the bottom of his chest. He leaned back against a tree, suddenly feeling all the fight leave his body.

"Aw, come on, Becs. Don't look at me like that. I know this situation is crazy, and I can't begin to imagine what's going through your head right now, seeing me again like this after all these years. But I promise you, I'm on your side here. And no matter what, I'd never hurt you. Ever." He ran one hand through his hair, suddenly conscious of all the white that had crept into it over the years. Then he glanced down at his chest and arms, feeling almost self-conscious about the physique he'd worked so hard to build. "I'm still the same guy you used to spar and joke around with back when we were younger. Only a whole lot older and in slightly different packaging."

As he watched, something softened in the lines of her face. Her shoulders relaxed slightly. But still her hands didn't drop.

"I'm not going anywhere with those men," she said.

"Of course you're not!" He chuckled without even meaning to at how ludicrous a thought that even was. Then he winced, as fire flashed in the depths of her eyes. She'd always hated being laughed at.

"You told me to go with them." She leveled the words at him like blows.

"No, I didn't! I told you to go around to the side of the van and fall flat on your face."

"You never *told* me to fall down. You just kept making stupid, Seth-like comments about how clumsy I was and that I was likely to fall down—"

"Because I was signaling to you that I needed you out of the line of fire. I needed you to get around the van, drop to the ground, so I could take them out without risking you getting shot. But I could hardly telegraph my plans in front of them. So I was trusting that you'd get what I was saying." His voice turned hoarse in his throat. "How could you not get that? What? Did you think I was just randomly insulting you, while your life was in danger, like some arrogant jerk?"

She raised her hands to her face. Her fingers pressed into the corners of her eyes, like she was fighting back tears. *Oh, wow.* She had. She'd been terrified, and in danger, and for some reason thought he was actually taking potshots at her. His head shook.

What happened, Rebecca? What happened to you? What happened to us?

In all the years she'd lived as a smiling face in his footlocker and as a memory at the corner of his mind, he'd focused on the good times. The mornings they'd gone jogging around the base together before anyone else was awake. The infectious laugh that would slip through her lips when he managed to surprise her. The way her fingers would brush against his arm.

But now, that final time he'd seen her, that painful moment he'd tried to forget, filled his mind in blaring sound and color. How she'd stood, just inside the shelter of the school archway, while the rain poured down around him. Smudgy lines of makeup making her eyes look even bigger. Her hair twisted around her head like something off a movie screen. And wearing some sparkling, extraordinary getup that had blown his mind and made him forget how words worked.

What are you doing here? Her eyes had narrowed. *You missed me getting the trophy.*

She'd been angry. Hurt. He hadn't known why.

He'd looked down at his feet. *I just enlisted.*

An engine rumbled in the distance. The van was leaving. Rebecca's fingers were still hiding her face.

His soldier's mind reminded him that she was the stepsister of a man who'd stolen government secrets. The fact that Black Talon mercenaries had come after her and Seth had blown up the road to her property meant she was somehow involved, whether she knew it or not. And his own CO had suggested he simply take her to Timmins and let the police handle it. Yet, for one brief moment, all his heart could see was his former best friend—frightened, overwhelmed and desperately needing someone to wrap their arms around her, pull her into their chest and hold her tightly.

Even if right now that person couldn't be him.

He stepped forward and reached for her hands. "I'm sorry. A long time ago, we had such an amazing connection. It was like we could read each other's minds. It was wrong of me to just assume you'd get what I was saying back there or what I was asking you to do."

She let him peel her hands away from her face. Her eyes were dark and brimming with questions.

"You didn't even tell me it was you," she said.

I was hoping you'd recognized me. I was hoping you'd know.

Maybe he'd even been hoping on some level that she'd never forgotten him just like he'd never forgotten her.

"I'm sorry," he said again. Her fingers fluttered in his. But she didn't pull away. "My real name is Zack Keats. I dropped the 'Biggs' when I enlisted. Keats was my mother's maiden name, my middle name and the last name of the uncle and aunt who raised me. I was the last of their family tree. I am a sergeant with the Canadian Armed Forces. Trust me, this is hardly the way I wanted this reunion to go and there's so much I want to tell you that I can't. But ask me any question you want, and I promise that even if I can't give you an answer, I will not lie to you."

She stepped back and pulled her hands away. Then she crossed her arms, leveled a steady, unflinching gaze at him and asked him the one question she'd know he'd never be able to answer. The one question he'd spent his whole adult life hoping no civilian would ever ask him:

"Are you with special ops?"

Zack didn't answer her. He didn't need to. The split-second flash of alarm in his eyes was all the confirmation she needed. In a nanosecond, his facade was calm again, expressionless, like that of a man who'd worked very hard at learning how to hide everything he really thought and felt so very deep down inside, so that it never came close to hitting the surface.

"The Canadian Forces special operations are highly classified," Zack said, almost mechanically.

"I know." *Just how I know that if you are special forces, you won't be able to tell me.* "But would it be okay if I told you a story?"

His eyebrows rose. "Go ahead."

"When I was a teenager my best friend, Zack, was a total genius. When it came to puzzles and figuring things out, his brain just seemed to work twice as fast as everyone else's." She watched as Zack swallowed hard. "My friend Zack told me once that his life's goal was to join the Canadian special forces.

Showed me all this research he'd managed to do about them. He had a binder of it. A literal three-ring binder. He took it that seriously. I never forgot that about him. So, over the years, I kept my ears open for news of the Canadian Forces special ops task force, especially when I was working on projects overseas. I always wondered if he'd made it and if my friend Zack was now one of those brave, unknown people secretly keeping the world safe."

His eyes were locked on hers, filled with words she knew he wouldn't be able to say. For a brief moment, the sheer pride she felt swelling inside her blocked out every other question in her mind. *No matter how upset and frustrated I am right now, I hope you know just how insanely impressed I am with you, too.*

Then she looked away and started walking back toward the direction of the road. He matched her pace.

"Then again," she added, "he was only eighteen at the time. He'd be in his late thirties now and getting close to forty. And how many people actually grow up to become exactly the man they'd always said they'd be?"

Certainly nobody else I've ever known. The forest floor crunched under their feet. Zack pulled his phone from his pocket, frowned, then slid it back.

"How about your stepbrother?" Zack asked. "What did he turn out to be?"

"Seth?" She blinked. Why did Zack want to know about him? He couldn't still be sore over how bad Seth had treated him. "What about him? He works in computers. We never talk."

There were handcuffs on Zack's belt, tucked under his sweatshirt, but still they jangled just a little as he walked.

"I overheard the phone conversation you had in my truck," she added. "I didn't set out to eavesdrop, but I'm a videographer and my truck is wired for video and sound. Who were you talking to and why did you tell them you were bringing me in?"

"That was my commanding officer, Major Jeff Lyons. I'd told you I was going to call him. I was just telling him that I was going to escort you to the police station in Timmins."

"Why does that require handcuffs and a gun?" She shot him a sideways glance. "You made it sound like you were going to drag me there against my will."

"Those aren't for you. They're for in case we run into trouble on our way there. The police want to talk to you about something, and he wanted to make sure I was going to remain professional and not accidentally compromise an active investigation because of our past friendship. I might've gotten a little emphatic about it."

"What kind of open investigation?" she pressed. "Why does the police want to talk to me?"

"Telling you that could compromise the police's ability to question you."

"Okay, but is it safe to assume it's linked to the fact that someone blew up the road?"

"I can't tell you about that."

"How about Ivan and Dmitry?"

He ran his hand over the back of his neck in a gesture so familiar it rattled something at the edges of her heart.

"I think it's safe to assume you're going to remember the tattoo those men had and look it up online," he said, carefully. She nodded. "When you do, you'll find references to a major Eastern European crime syndicate, which translates roughly as 'Black Talon.' Basically they steal things, smuggle things, sell things illegally and kill people, and to make matters worse there are warring factions within Black Talon violently fighting for supremacy over the group. You'll also discover they tattoo themselves with the name of their first confirmed kill. So technically, those two men would be The-Man-Who-Killed-Ivan and The-Man-Who-Killed-Dmitry, but I've been mentally calling them Ivan and Dmitry for short, too. But what I don't know is why two members of Black Talon would be in Canada or why they just tried to kidnap you. I wouldn't even want to guess. As you probably noticed I tried fishing for information a bit, trying to see if they knew who I was and if they'd been hired for money."

"Could you understand what they were saying?" she asked.

"Yup." He chuckled slightly. "Basically, it all came down to 'Shoot him!' and 'Take her!' and 'Stop acting like an idiot or I'll kill you.'"

They reached the road. It was empty. The kidnappers and their van were gone. They walked back toward her camper. Every inch of her skin seemed to tingle with electricity from being this close to him. The old, familiar smell of him filled her senses. *I'm frightened. I'm angry. I'm beyond frustrated that Zack won't give me answers. And my heart won't stop fluttering whenever he glances my way.*

She could now see the camper between the trees. She stopped walking and turned toward him. They stood there a moment, chest to chest, face-to-face, just inches apart in the dirt.

"Can you tell me one thing?" she asked. "Is your target the man who blew up the road? Or Black Talon? Or me?"

"None of you are my target." His hands swung wide above his head, as if he was trying to swat the horizon. "Like I told you before, I'm not on assignment right now. I'm on vacation. On leave. This is my holiday. I actually need to report back to base in less than two days for overseas deployment." His arms dropped back down to his side. "This morning I was camping at the side of a lake about an hour south of here, then I heard something on the news—which I'm guessing you haven't heard or you wouldn't be asking so many questions—and I figured you might need an old friend to talk to."

His hands parted slightly like he wanted to hug her but wasn't sure if he should.

"When you climbed out of the rocks, I didn't think you recognized me," he went on, "and I was trying to figure out how to tell you who I was when my commanding officer called and suggested I shouldn't."

"How did he know you were with me?" she asked.

"He guessed." He looked past her into the trees. "I have a very old news clipping about you winning that martial arts trophy taped inside my footlocker. Now, please stop asking me questions I can't answer. Just stop. Please. I'm already in trouble enough with my CO for potentially barging onto a gigantic mess for personal reasons."

A "mess" that involved foreign criminals, explosives and weapons.

"Just let me ask one more question, please, then I'll stop."

He ran both hands over his head. "Go ahead."

"Why is there a newspaper article about me in your locker?"

An article about the night you broke my heart?

His eyes glanced to the sky and his lips moved for a moment like he was praying.

"Because you changed my life, Rebecca." His eyes dropped to her face. "You believed in me and stuck by me when nobody else did. I'd never forgotten what it was like to walk into that gym, overweight, out of shape, feeling laughed at, and yet wanting to be better than I was. And you…sorry to be so blunt, but you were the cutest thing I'd ever seen and yet you walked right over and asked me to partner with you. You befriended me. You encouraged me. So yeah—" and here his voice rose, as if he was arguing with an opponent she couldn't see "—today when I realized you could be in trouble, and knew I'd followed your career just enough, and remembered your stories well enough, to know you might not be too far away, I came to find you. Because you had my back when nobody else did and I wanted to make sure I had yours now."

Her heart flipped in her chest, as if they'd been standing on the mats and he'd just grabbed her by the heels and tossed her end over end.

"But it was a mistake," he said. "Because there's something big going on and guys like me don't have the luxury of making personal decisions. Not where stuff like this is involved."

He stepped back, reached into his pocket and pulled out his phone. "Now that I've got a signal, I'm going to call my commanding officer again and tell him we just had some unwanted company. Do you need any help packing up your camper?"

She shook her head. "No, thanks, I'll be fine."

He walked her to her camper door, waited until she stepped inside and then dialed a number. She could hear his voice fading in the distance as he strode off through the trees. She sat down on her bunk and dropped her head into her hands, feeling as if she should pray but not even knowing how to start sorting out the scattered feelings of her heart.

Her gold martial arts trophy sat on the small shelf beside her bunk, on top of the glossy hardcover copy of General Arthur Miles's autobiography that someone on his staff had mailed her, she guessed out of courtesy, even though she and her mother weren't in it. Rebecca had never been close to her stepfather, which had probably disappointed Zack a bit when they were younger, considering how much he'd admired the man and how often Zack had hinted that he hoped she'd introduce them. It'd been odd being in the same family as someone whose name everyone seemed to know and yet she'd never personally felt close to, even though her mother had insisted she and Rebecca both change their last names to "Miles."

But the General had traveled frequently, and Seth's ability to make her feel unwelcome had tended to go into overdrive whenever his father was home on leave.

Rebecca stood up and started tidying, pushing things into drawers, shutting down her machines and locking things behind cupboard doors. Something rustled in the trees outside. Wind? No, there were footsteps in the forest outside.

"Hey, Zack?" she called. "I'm about ready to go."

No answer. The footsteps grew closer. Her pulse raced. Her hand reached for a kitchen knife. Then there was the click. The camper door swung open.

Her hand rose to her lips. The knife clattered to the floor.

"Hey there, Sis. Long time no see."

It was Seth.

FIVE

"Well, aren't you going to welcome me?" Seth Miles strode through the doorway of Rebecca's camper in jeans and a T-shirt. She blinked. He was thinner than he'd been the last time she saw him. His blond hair was longer, too. Blue eyes scanned the camper as if they were searching for something.

"Oh, wow. Hi." She gave Seth a quick hug, and was surprised to feel his lean arms actually clasp her back tightly. "What are you doing here?"

"Felt like camping." His grin was twitchy. "Can't believe you're still using this thing. I see you've converted my old bunk into a video editing suite."

"This is my home and my office now."

Had he just showed up and walked past Zack? Considering the past tension between them, it was hard to imagine they'd waved hello and nodded cordially. But Zack had apparently not felt the need to accompany him to her trailer, either.

Seth's eyes were still scanning her stuff. Her equipment was great for video editing, but probably nothing compared to the high-speed processing power Seth was used to. For a moment it looked like he was about to reach for her martial arts trophy. But then his hand diverted at the last moment and grabbed his father's autobiography. He flipped through it without even glancing at the pages. His shoulders were so tense she couldn't help but think of a bird of prey in need of a meal. "You're packing up?"

"Yes, I'm heading to Timmins." Her arms crossed in front of her chest. "So, what's going on, Seth? Don't even try to pretend this is some spontaneous social call."

"The way I see it, you're the one with secrets." Seth dropped the book and crossed his own arms, mirroring her stance. "You want to tell me what your old friend Zack is doing standing around outside? I didn't even recognize him at first, until I walked up and introduced myself. Even then he was hardly talkative. Please tell me you two aren't a couple. I always knew he had a pretty serious crush on you when we were kids. But he was never good enough for you."

Heat rose to her cheeks. She turned away and pressed her cool palms against her face. Zack had a crush on her? Even if he had, any romantic attraction was sure to be long gone. "Zack's in the military now—"

Seth snorted.

She turned back. "Don't be like that. I know you never thought much of authority figures, but Zack worked very hard to get to where he is and I for one am proud of him."

Now Seth's arrogant grin turned into a grimace. Something she'd said had obviously bothered him. Trying to have a straight-up conversation with Seth when he was like this was like trying to tack down a snake. She'd lost track of the number of times he'd practically forced his way into her room when they'd been teenagers, only to just sit there, not talking about whatever was going on in his brain. He must've noticed the blocked road, even though he hadn't asked her about it yet. She also needed to fill him in on the explosives and on Black Talon.

But while Zack wasn't willing to tell her what was happening, Seth might. Zack wasn't back from his phone call, which gave her a very small window of time to find things out from Seth. She wasn't going to waste a second of it.

"Now, come on," she said. "Tell me the truth. Zack told me that there's something big on the news and that police want to talk to me. So if you're suddenly showing up here now, you obviously know what it is."

She didn't know what response to expect, but it certainly wasn't the one that she got. Seth laughed—a long, loud bark that sounded equal parts angry and relieved. "So, Zack never told you *why* the police want to talk to you?"

"No," she admitted. "I was hoping you'd tell me."

"Just be glad you didn't marry Zack. You'd have obviously turned out just as clueless as your mother and mine."

She didn't really know anything about Seth's mother, only that she'd suddenly abandoned Seth and his father when Seth was twelve and he'd apparently never heard from her since. She hadn't been in the autobiography, either.

"Okay, truth is a few weeks ago somebody published a website online about the General," Seth said. "Anonymously, of course. Probably because the General's been tipped to become a senator soon. Anyway, someone created a blog claiming he was a philanderer and cheated on our mothers. I'm guessing you never read it. I emailed you a link." He shrugged and looked down at the floor. "Well, it's all over the news and now police want to talk to us about it."

None of which explained anything that had happened to her so far today.

"So, someone is muckraking gossip about your father?" Considering the heartache her mother had gone through with Rebecca's father having disappeared from their lives before Rebecca was even born, it was disappointing to think her mother would've then married a man who was unfaithful, on top of being unavailable. The General's marriage history was hardly a secret, although it was rarely commented on in his news coverage, as it had nothing to do with his military record. Seth's mother had abandoned them. Rebecca's mother had died. He was now on his third. "Honestly, I don't get why anyone would bother writing salacious garbage like that, or why anyone would bother reading it."

Let alone why European mobsters would be after her.

"Well, let's just head out and we can go talk to the police together. Hopefully this'll all be cleared up soon." He leaped out of the camper. "Brothers and sisters should stick together."

She followed him out. Zack was still nowhere in sight.

"Where did Zack go?"

"He walked down the road to take a phone call. Said he needed some privacy."

Seth was practically running to her truck.

"Where's your vehicle?" she asked.

"Oh, I parked it on the road. Road's all blocked off just south of here. Weirdest thing. So I left it there and walked up to find you." Seth opened the front door of her truck. For a moment she thought he was opening it for her. But he jumped into the driver's seat.

"Hang on!" She stepped into the open space between the door and the seat. "One, you're not driving my truck, so get out. Two, stop talking like a car salesman and be straight with me. I'm not even sure I believe any of your story. Somebody tried to kill me. Somebody tried to kill Zack. I was nearly kidnapped—"

"What do you mean you were kidnapped?" Seth froze. "When? By who?"

"Eastern European gangsters. Zack saved my life."

Seth reached up, flipped the sun visor down and pulled out her spare key.

"Go find Zack and get out of here. Go to a police station, or his base, or wherever. Just get somewhere safe, and stay there."

"What's really going on, Seth? You're caught up in this, aren't you?" She should've known better than to believe that stupid story about some blog about his father for a second.

Seth wouldn't look at her. "I've got to go."

"Not in my truck you don't." Her hand grabbed the sunroof. She stepped up onto the running board. "Tell me what's happening."

"You wouldn't get it." He set his jaw. "You never did."

What's he talking about? Her eyes scanned the tree line. *Where's Zack really?* Seth was clenching the steering wheel so tightly his knuckles were white. Her fingers stared at the gunpowder stains on his fingertips. *Help me, Lord.* A feeling like ice poured through her veins.

"You're the one who blew up the road." Her other hand grabbed the steering wheel. If only Zack had told her. He had to have known. "Why, because you were trying to block my property off from the main road? Because you were going to hide out here? Your stunt nearly killed me."

"I was trying to protect you! Just like I always did. You were just too blind to see it!"

A look she'd rarely seen flashed in her stepbrother's eyes. Defiance. *Pride.* She'd only seen this look on his face once before. Just once. The night of the sports banquet. After Zack had stood her up, Seth had found her in her bedroom, still in her fancy dress, crying her eyes out. He'd stood there silently for a moment as if he didn't know what to do, looking proud and confused. Then he'd shrugged and said, *Stand up. I'll take ya. You might as well get your trophy.*

"I'm done talking about this." He turned the key in the ignition. Her truck started. "I never meant to hurt you. Whether you choose to believe that or not."

Seth's foot hit the gas. The truck lurched forward a few feet on the uneven ground. Her arm felt like it was being wrenched from her body. She held on tight. "Stop!"

"Rebecca! Let go!" Seth panicked. "Get off the truck! You're going to hurt yourself!"

Her feet stayed planted on the running board. The truck was rolling slowly through the forest, dragging her camper behind it. "I'm going to hurt myself? You're the one stealing my truck and my camper."

"I don't have a choice. Just know, I never meant for you to get hurt."

Seth hit the gas.

The smell of the forest floor filled Zack's nostrils. Dirt pressed against his face. His head ached. Darkness swam in and out before his eyes as if they couldn't quite focus. He couldn't believe he'd actually been knocked out. Zack blinked hard. Then he crouched, pressed one palm into the ground and listened.

Silence. Beyond the sound of wind brushing through the trees.

One moment he'd been on the phone with Jeff. He'd called Major Lyons on his personal line to fill him in about Black Talon. His commanding officer had been so upset, he'd almost been yelling. Not angry exactly, but more like very loudly worried. Both Seth's theft and Black Talon were already the source of two different internal security-breach investigations. The idea of them somehow being linked meant multiple breaches on multiple levels and the kind of perfect storm that could ground the careers of everyone involved until it was sorted.

Added to that, Zack had hardly been able to hear the major. The connection had been terrible and kept cutting out, plus Jeff's voice had echoed, like he'd been calling from the bottom of a very deep underground stairwell.

And then, something had hit him.

Zack groaned. His gun was gone, as was the one he'd lifted from Ivan. But he still had his handcuffs tucked inside his sweatshirt. His eyes searched the ground. There was a large rubber bullet by his feet, the kind shot from the type of air gun used to subdue protests. He'd been watching the road like a hawk and hadn't heard a vehicle approaching. So whoever attacked him must've been hiding in the trees, waiting to take a shot, and apparently using whatever kind of weapons he'd been able to get on the black market.

At least they hadn't wanted Zack dead. He'd been so focused on securing the road, he hadn't secured the forest. Not that securing endless trees was the easiest thing for one man to do.

Still, it's my fault for still thinking of these woods as my home turf, in good old Northern Ontario, instead of realizing I'm now in hostile territory.

He started back down the road toward Rebecca's camper, striding quickly but silently, praying hard he'd find her safe. None of this would've happened if he hadn't let himself become distracted thinking about her.

Yes, he'd had no backup, hadn't expected a shooter in the woods. Plus Jeff had been deeply concerned, and the connection had been so terrible he'd been straining to hear him. All of which had contributed to his failure. But none of that changed the fact that he'd let this thing with Rebecca become personal. Something about the curve of her smile, the scent of her hair, the way his skin almost shivered whenever her hand brushed his—just being around Rebecca again made him feel as if there was still some leftover youthful attraction for her trapped somewhere deep inside him and he didn't know how to shut it off.

If Rebecca got hurt, or worse, because he hadn't kept his feelings in check, he'd never forgive himself.

He heard the truck engine. Voices shouting. Then Rebecca's screams seem to split the air. He ran toward the sound. "Hang on! I'm coming!"

The truck crashed through the trees toward him. Rebecca was hanging out of the open driver's-side door. Her feet were braced on the running board. One hand clenched the edge of the open sunroof. Her other hand fought for the steering wheel. It was one of the craziest, gutsiest, most foolhardy things he'd ever seen.

Hang on, Rebecca, I'm coming.

Tree branches smacked against her body. Zack leaped into the path of the truck and raised both arms. The truck didn't stop.

"Zack!" Rebecca shouted. "It's Seth! Don't let him get away!"

Oh, I don't intend to.

But the truck was still moving and Rebecca was still hanging on to the side. If he had to get hit by a truck to stop Seth and save Rebecca's life, he would. Seth's eyes met Zack's through the windshield. The traitor's eyes narrowed. Then Seth hit the brakes. The truck slowed to a stop. *Thank You, God.* Zack ran for Rebecca and reached for her hand. "Let go. It's okay. I've got this."

Seth hit the gas. The truck flew forward again and swerved out onto the road. Zack threw himself backward and barely avoided getting sideswiped by the camper as it flew past. The truck was now picking up speed on the pavement. Zack dashed after them.

Then Seth wrenched the wheel from her grasp.

Rebecca flew backward onto the road. The camper swung wildly on the trailer hitch. Metal storage boxes and camping equipment flew off the back of the truck.

Prayer shot through Zack like lightning.

It was all going to hit her.

SIX

Rebecca was rolling. Bouncing. Tossed against the pavement like a rag doll. She could hear the screech of tires coming toward her and smell the stench of hot metal and gasoline. Then she felt a warm body land on top of hers, holding her down, protecting her from the equipment and debris as it rained down around them. She curled into a ball, felt the rush of wind over their bodies and heard the sound of tires screeching in the distance. Then she felt the slow, steady beat of Zack's heart.

He rolled off her. "You're okay."

She pulled herself up onto her hands and knees and stared down the road ahead. The tail end of the camper swerved wildly, fishtailing out from behind the speeding truck.

Then it was gone.

Her camper. Her truck. Her business. Her equipment. Her life.

Stolen by her arrogant bully of a stepbrother.

Her fists clenched and for a moment she didn't know whether to scream or cry.

"You're okay," Zack said again. He crouched beside her. His hand lightly touched the small of her back. "You're strong. You're tough. You're going to get through this. I promise."

She glanced up at him and blinked back the tears threatening to spill down her cheek. How did he still know the exact right thing to say? He'd remembered that whenever she'd been tossed and thrown and felt like a failure the last thing she wanted was sympathy, and the first thing she needed was the reminder she was strong enough to get up and keep fighting—even as she could see worry for her well-being echoing in the depths of his eyes.

She wiped her hand across her face. Then she reached for his hand and let him help her up. "Thank you."

"You took that roll well. Kept your head tucked in. Any injuries I should be aware of?"

Now he sounded exactly like her old sparring partner.

"Thank you," she said again. They stood. For a moment she let her hand linger in his. *Thanks for handling it this way. Like we're equals. Two warriors. Two fighters. Instead of reminding me that you're a special ops sergeant, and I'm the fool who just got her truck stolen.* "I'm okay. More bumps and bruises to add to the last set. But I'm okay."

She pulled her hand away. He was standing there, his arms apart like he was waiting for her to fall into his chest for a hug. But they weren't sparring partners anymore. They weren't even friends. He was nothing but a man she used to know, who'd kept something from her, and it had just cost her everything she owned.

"You knew about Seth from the very beginning. You knew he was the one who'd blown up the road."

Zack held her gaze and didn't look away. "I did."

"So, what did he do?"

"It might be unwise to tell you as it could jeopardize the police investigation when they question you."

"I don't care!" She waved both hands through the air. "I've been attacked by gangsters. I've nearly been kidnapped. Seth just lied to my face and stole everything I own, leaving me stranded." She reached for his hands and held them in both of hers. "Leaving *us* stranded, and I'm guessing that our lives are still in danger. So you can't have this both ways, Zack. Not anymore. You can't be my old best friend who I trust implicitly one moment, and then Mister Secret Ops keeping me in the dark the next. I don't know if 'on a need-to-know basis' is a thing you guys actually say, but this is a need-to-know basis. And I need to know."

He stared at her for a long moment, like he didn't know if he wanted to kiss her or throw both his hands up in exasperation again. Either way, she could feel a flush creep into her cheeks. She dropped his hands.

He ran his hand over his jaw. A grin spread across his face.

"Need-to-know basis," he muttered. Then he slid his hands into his pockets. "Well, then, let's walk and talk. Because if we have any hope of flagging down help it won't be on this road. I still have my wallet and handcuffs, but no phone and no gun. How about you? Is there anything useful in the stuff that just got tossed off the back of your camper?"

She shook her head. "No. Sadly. It's all heavy-duty winter gear, and I don't even have my wallet."

"I left my bag under the passenger seat in your truck," he said, "and your minilaptop in the glove compartment. I'm presuming they're still there?"

"As far as I know," she said. He frowned. "I presume that's a bad thing?"

"Yup, pretty bad."

They started walking. Zack didn't seem in much of a hurry to start talking. Or maybe he just didn't know where to start.

"Seth showed up at the camper as I was busy packing it up," she said. "Stupidly I let him get to my truck."

"He knocked me out while I was on the phone with my CO," Zack said. "We were both caught off guard, and you didn't know to distrust him."

True, but it was nice to hear him say it.

"Seth told me some big lie about how the General, Arthur Miles, my former stepfather, was up for a seat in the Senate and someone had anonymously posted this big blog about him online, accusing him of cheating on both of our mothers."

"That's true," Zack said.

She blinked. "What part of it?"

"All of it," Zack said. "General Miles is expected to be appointed to the Senate this fall. Somebody did create a pretty distasteful blog about him recently, accusing him of philandering. It was disappointing. Our military is under enough pressure without someone stirring up twenty-or thirty-year-old gossip about the marital life of one of our top generals. Nobody likes it when somebody tries to drag down a hero. In my opinion, we need more people in the Senate like General Miles. Not fewer."

"Seth was telling the *truth*? Criminals want to kidnap me because someone is muckraking gossip about a man who was briefly my stepfather?"

Zack didn't answer. He didn't need to. The answer was in the cut of his jaw and the set of his shoulders.

No, that wasn't why police wanted to question her at all.

"Please, Zack." Her hand slid onto his arm. "We're alone in the middle of nowhere. My life's been threatened. Your life's been threatened. Seth fed me some ridiculous sideshow story to distract me. I don't see how keeping me in the dark is going to make either of us any safer. You used to be the one guy I trusted more than anyone else on the planet. So please, tell me straight, what's really going on?"

Zack stopped walking.

"Do you think it's easy for me to trust someone who won't trust me?" he asked. His tone was gentle and somehow that made his words even harder to hear. "You know what we call people who refuse to let us help them? *Liabilities.* You make it sound like this is all one-sided, Becs. Like I'm the bad guy here. But you don't listen to me when I try to have your back. You don't let me protect you. You ran from me, more than once. You throw yourself into danger like you don't have any other choice. You eavesdropped on my conversation and when you heard something that upset you, instead of asking me about it, you attacked me with bug spray—which was really clever, I'll admit. You're brave and I respect that. But that trust we used to have? We built it. Through every time you let me toss you on the mat and every time you let me aim a sparring blow at your face. You trusted I wouldn't hurt you. You trusted I'd protect you. And now?" He shrugged. "Now, I wouldn't spar with you, because you'd be so busy running around in circles and tossing wild punches it wouldn't be safe. For either of us."

There was a sharp pain in her chest. But not like Zack's words had pierced her. More like there'd already been something jagged caught deep inside her, and she'd gotten used to the feel of it, and now, it was being pulled out.

"You're right." She let out a long breath. "And I'm sorry. But I don't know what to do about it or how to fix it."

"Me, neither."

She stared at his face for a moment and tried to imagine all the days in his life that she'd missed. His first time in uniform. The mornings he'd gone running with his unit. The evenings he'd spent alone in the gym lifting weights. The moment he'd found out he'd been selected for special ops. The bullets and explosions he'd run through. The helicopters he'd jumped out of. The people he'd carried to safety.

All the nights he'd lain awake, under foreign skies, praying to the God he believed in.

She stepped toward him. His arms opened. And suddenly she felt her hands sliding up around his neck. His arms slid around her waist and settled into the small of her back. Then he lifted her up off the ground, just like he used to, and they held each other tightly for one long moment, as if they were trying to squeeze a thousand missing hugs into one. Then he set her back down. They kept walking.

"Seth worked for a civilian computer firm that was updating government computers," Zack said. "He stole something from one of the military computers he had access to. I honestly don't know what it was, because whatever it was is above my pay grade. But it might be the computer program I took off him that's currently sitting on your laptop. But sadly, we lost that when Seth stole the truck."

Suddenly the way Seth had been eyeing her equipment made sense. While they weren't as high-grade as he was probably used to, he'd essentially just stolen a computer lab and video studio on wheels. A whole bunch of questions leaped to the tip of her tongue. She didn't ask any of them. It was more that she was too numb to be angry or shocked.

"It's all over the news, as you can imagine," he went on. "The son of a military hero and soon-to-be senator potentially stealing government secrets is a pretty huge deal. Like I told you, I was camping while on leave, saw it on the news and so drove straight up to make sure you were okay. I never imagined Seth would be up here. The news said it looked like he was heading southwest to a big city center like Seattle or Los Angeles."

He was quiet again for a moment, as if he was weighing words in his head and trying to decide whether or not to say them.

"Your brother is also accused of shooting an unidentified woman in an Ottawa park," Zack said finally. "She was shot in the stomach and is currently in critical condition."

Now the dull feeling inside her started to shift like an earthquake. "Seth's not a killer."

"He's wanted for attempted murder," Zack said. "He's also wanted for theft and suspicion of treason."

Hot tears pushed their way into the corners of her eyes. Seth was arrogant, rude and a bully. She still didn't know what to make of the odd claim that he'd tried to protect her, and she could easily believe he was guilty of stealing something from a military computer. But killing a woman in cold blood? Seth's eyes flashed through her memory, filled with both defiance and pain.

The sun beat down on their limbs. The pavement felt heavy under her feet. After a while they left a small road and turned onto a larger rural highway. Very few vehicles passed them and even fewer slowed. She let Zack take the lead in flagging down anyone for help. Not surprisingly, Zack was incredibly cautious. He positioned himself between her and the road, and more than once at the sound of an engine stepped in front of her and urged her to step back into the trees.

Finally, he flagged down a transport truck hauling cattle. The northern Quebecois driver didn't speak much English, and Rebecca's French was shaky beyond what she could remember from reading the sides of cereal boxes, so she had no choice but to let Zack take the lead in negotiating passage. Finally they climbed into the cab with a cheerful, white-haired driver, who introduced himself as "Bon Jacques."

"It's a joke," Zack explained, as he squeezed his large frame in between Rebecca and the passenger door. "See, *'un bon jack'* in Quebecois French is like how we'd say in English, 'He's a good guy.'"

She smiled at the driver, extended her hand and used the only French she could remember besides the words for "many" and "cornflakes." *"Merci."*

Jacques nodded, his grin wide. "Welcome." Then he pulled out a bottle of water and offered it to them. Rebecca took a long sip and handed it to Zack. They drove. The comforting smell of barnyard animals and hay filled the air. Zack slid his arm along the back of the seat. His fingers brushed her shoulder.

"What did you tell him?" she asked.

"That I'm a member of the Canadian Armed Forces, our vehicle was stolen and we need a ride. He's not heading to Timmins, but has agreed to drop us off at the first gas station we pass."

Right. So that would make everything else "need to know." The radio played music in French. Zack borrowed a phone from Jacques and when he got a cell signal placed a quick call to 911 to report that her vehicle had been stolen and that Seth Miles had taken it. No doubt that would send Ontario police scrambling. He also put in a quick call to his commanding officer and left a brief message: Seth had attacked them. Seth had the laptop. He'd check in again soon.

Zack hung up, then opened a map-based website and entered some coordinates. The truck rumbled down a narrow highway. The seats bounced beneath them. Jacques started humming along to the radio under his breath.

Then Zack placed another call. The phone display read "Shield Trust."

The overseas technical charity? She'd heard of them. In fact, their name was on the list of the documentary projects she hoped to tackle one day. Mark Shields had come from a very wealthy background and given it up to found a technology-based charity that helped local groups in developing countries with innovative technical solutions.

Sounded as if Zack had gotten his friend's voice mail.

"Hey, Mark. Long story, but I'm in Canada. Your neighborhood actually. Sorry for the short notice, but is there anyone at the island house now? I've hit a major snag and might need a place to regroup for a couple of hours. Love to Katie." He hung up.

Rebecca raised an eyebrow. "Regroup?"

Zack sighed. Then he leaned his head in toward her. His voice dropped to a whisper. "I was really hoping I'd get through to Jeff. He was really upset during our last phone call and I couldn't make out half of what he was saying. Considering we're not that far from my friend Mark's house, and everything that's gone on in the past twenty-four hours, I thought it might not be the worst idea to head there and call Jeff. It was just a thought. But Mark might not even be in the country and it probably makes more sense to go straight to the closest police station."

She nodded slowly. "I saw the company name on your phone. I've heard of them."

"Mark's an old friend of mine. I used to be his bodyguard a very, very long time ago. My grandmother knew his grandmother and set it up. Back then, Mark was just an angry kid who needed someone to run away from. And I was that someone. We became tight. Hang on—"

He sat up straight and held out the phone. A faint red dot was blipping at the corner of an unmarked lake. "I think we've found your truck."

Zack stared at the blinking dot and traced the route in his mind. Looked like Seth had taken an unmarked, unpaved dirt road that was maybe twenty minutes ahead on their left.

Jacques's truck would never be able to make it and Zack wasn't about to ask. But Jacques should be able to drop him off within hiking distance.

Rebecca leaned into him and stared down at the phone. Her body nestled into his shoulder. Dark hair fell over her face. Even lost and bedraggled and after everything she'd been through, there was something captivating about her.

It was terribly distracting.

"You put a tracker in my truck?" she asked.

"No, there's a GPS tracker in my bag, which I left under the front seat of your truck, and another in my cell phone. The fact they're both showing the same location is a very good sign." He leaned past her, showed the screen to Jacques and explained the situation in French. Then he leaned back. "Okay, I'm going to get Jacques to drop me off there, hike in and retrieve our stuff. Hopefully I'll even stop Seth while I'm at it. I've asked Jacques to drop you off at the first town he drives through. There's about fifty dollars cash in my wallet, which you can have. Plus a credit card for emergencies—"

"No." She shook her head. "You're not just leaving me alone in a truck with a stranger who I can't even talk the same language as."

"Jacques is a good man." Zack's voice

dropped. His arm slipped down Rebecca's back. He pulled her in closer. "I trust him. He'll get you there safely."

"But what if Black Talon or someone else attacks us on the road?" she asked. "What if I'm grabbed in whatever small town he drops me off in?"

Did she think she'd be any safer tracking Seth down?

The last thing he needed right now was a distraction and a spare person to worry about. Retrieving the stolen material and stopping potential terrorists had to be the top priority.

"That's not very likely." He pulled his arm away, then crossed his arms in front of his chest. "This is small-town Ontario. It's hardly a foreign war zone."

Her lips were set. Her head was shaking. Was he going to have to force her to stay here in the truck?

The phone began to ring. He glanced at the screen. Blocked number. He glanced at Jacques, who shrugged as if giving Zack permission to answer it. "Hello?"

"Name, rank and service number?" The voice belonged to Jeff.

Zack rattled them off. The major sighed. "Location?"

"Highway Eleven. About twenty-five minutes from South Porcupine. Thirty from the presumed target and the cache."

"The target and cache have been located?"

"Yes, sir."

"Are you on a secure line?"

"No, sir. But there are some things I do need to brief you on that can't wait. I've got a good idea where we can find both Seth and the laptop containing whatever he stole."

Another sigh. This one sounded far less relieved. "There's been a lot of pressure coming down from the higher-ups, even more than you'd expect under the circumstances. I don't know where it's coming from, but it's been suggested I get you back at base and soon."

"Are you revoking my leave?" Zack's eyes glanced back at the screen. The flashing dot disappeared.

"I haven't received that order, yet," he said. "But, the media is now reporting that the woman Seth Miles shot is dead. They're still not reporting her name. But unofficially, she's probably a member of the same organization as the unpleasant criminal duo you ran into earlier today. Not a new one, either. Looks like she's been working as a member of the Ontario Provincial Police for over two years. Uncertain how she gained that access or where her immigration papers even came from. Her police academy qualifications were fake."

Seth's victim was a Black Talon operative? He didn't know what was more alarming, that Black Talon might have recruited Seth, or that a member of Black Talon could've been hiding inside the Ontario Provincial Police. Either way, that made it slightly more plausible that Seth hadn't been the one who'd actually shot her.

"The media is now reporting that a warrant has been issued for Rebecca's arrest," Jeff went on. "But I haven't been able to get external confirmation of that. Seems there's equal doses of news and misinformation on the airwaves right now, thanks to some anonymous sources. I recommend you take her to a safe location and I'll arrange transport for the both of you back to base."

"Copy that." Zack's eyes glanced back at the screen. Still no flashing dot. They were over eight hours' drive from his base and there weren't many places for a helicopter to land in forest this dense. But if the dot on the phone had meant what he thought it had, he was so incredibly close to the stolen computer program he could have it safely retrieved within the hour.

"Until the source of the internal breach is

isolated," Jeff said, "it's best to assume that no lines are secure, and that no one can be trusted."

Which was code for: *And I know even more I'm not telling you.*

So, Northern Ontario really was a hostile environment until all this was settled. Anyone with sufficient technical know-how could be monitoring cell phone calls, and the police had already been infiltrated by at least one Black Talon mercenary. Could he really just leave Rebecca in the care of Jacques, have him drop her off at the closest town and expect her to be all right? Zack ran his palm over his eyes. *Lord, I don't know what's going on. But I could really use Your wisdom.*

"So basically trust absolutely no one, is that what you're saying?" Zack asked.

The phone line went dead. Zack couldn't tell if it was from the cell signal dying or if his commanding officer had hung up. He glanced at Rebecca. "Well, looks like we're sticking together for now."

"Did you just say, 'Trust no one'?"

Ah. He probably shouldn't have said that within her earshot. "Basically. But don't worry about it. What matters is that we're heading to your truck together. But you've got to let me take the lead here. I don't want you running at

Seth the moment we find him. We know he's armed. We don't know if he's alone. We don't even know what he's capable of. Got it?"

"Got it," Rebecca said. She leaned forward and tightened her laces. "Although, if you really are trusting no one, are you even sure you can trust your CO? How do you know he isn't part of this? How do you know he hasn't been feeding you misinformation or trying to lead you into a trap?"

Zack could feel his jaw drop. What kind of question was that? A retort flew to the tip of his tongue, but when he glanced at her face, he could tell she was serious. "Because I trust him. There are some people I trust without question. He's one of them. It's as simple as that."

Jacques dropped them off at the side of the road beside an unmarked dirt track and refused to take the money Zack offered him. Zack's chest ached to realize Jacques would probably see Rebecca's picture flashed across the news later in the day and realize he'd given a ride to a criminal suspect, but as he looked into the older man's kindly, smiling eyes Zack realized he didn't know what to say to reassure him.

The truck left. A sigh left his body.

"He went out of his way to help us," Zack said, "but he doesn't know who we are and what we're in the middle of. If we recover what Seth stole right now, Jacques might've just helped save countless lives and thwart an international criminal plot, and he'll never know it."

They started walking through the woods.

"Am I right in gathering that General Miles kept a lot of secrets from your mother?" he asked, after a long moment. If he was honest the fact that Rebecca had questioned his trust in Jeff rattled him just a bit. "Is that part of why secrets bother you so much?"

"Yeah," she said. "General Miles was definitely very hard to get to know or feel close to. Maybe that's just a side effect of the job. But it didn't help that my mother's relationship with my biological father was shrouded in secrecy. I wasn't even allowed to ask who he was or where he'd gone, even though she spent my whole childhood anxiously waiting to hear from him. Then suddenly she'd given up waiting for him, married General Miles instead and things got even worse. She never knew where in the world my stepfather was or what he was doing. It's part of why she got so hooked on the prescription pills that eventually killed her. The uncertainty drove her crazy. She couldn't handle the secrets. I lived with the General for about five years, my mother lived with him for seven, and still, I don't know who he really was."

That might've been the most he'd ever heard her say about General Miles. As teenagers, she'd always changed the topic or just gone quiet whenever he'd babbled enthusiastically about the General's war record or the operations he could be deployed on. The idea anyone would be anything other than thrilled about living with a decorated military hero hadn't really occurred to him back then, and he definitely wouldn't have tolerated hearing anyone bad-mouth someone in the Armed Forces, which was probably part of what'd driven his tensions with Seth. With two parents who'd died in the service, and both an uncle and aunt who'd served, teenage Zack had had a pretty idealized, almost naive view of the men and women in uniform, instead of realizing they were just as human as everybody else.

Certainly none of the men or women he served with now were perfect.

"I know you hate that I'm keeping things from you," he said, including the fact that there was a warrant out for her arrest and that police had been infiltrated by Black Talon. "And honestly, I don't blame you. Nobody *likes* it when somebody is keeping secrets. I sure don't. It still irks me whenever I can tell there's something going on in my unit that I don't know about. Because I see all the signs—the glances, the closed doors, the way people hide the screen when checking their cell phones—and I wonder about it just like anyone else. Are we about to be deployed? Is there a new terrorist threat? Is someone planning a surprise party? Remember, I still don't know what Seth stole.

"But I've accepted that part of my job. I've accepted that in this gossip-filled, knowledge-driven culture, I don't get to know everything. Some things are still private. Some secrets aren't mine to know."

They kept walking. He was thankful she was listening, even if he wasn't sure how to put his thoughts into words. He'd never actually talked to anyone about this before.

"Go on," she said.

"I just kept a pretty big secret from Jacques, while he might've helped me achieve my goals," he added. "That happens more often than you'd think. There are men and women all over the world who gave me a ride, or offered me a drink of water, or bartered with me for a piece of equipment I needed, or walked with me into enemy territory, or tipped me off to where hostiles were hiding—*risked their lives*—but who are never going to know the difference they made and what they were a part of. Because I'm the only person who knows, and it would put them in danger if I told them. That's the part of keeping secrets that gets to me. Not the fact that my superiors can't tell me everything—like I said, I've accepted that—but the fact that I can't ever tell people how incredibly grateful I am for the huge difference they've made."

Rebecca didn't answer and he felt foolish almost immediately for admitting what he had. That what he, Sergeant Zack Keats of special forces, found hardest about his job wasn't hostile elements, dangerous conditions or the physical toll the job took on his body. No, it was the fact that when he was safely home, after an operation, he couldn't go back to find some random man on a hillside or woman from a market to give them whatever money he had in his wallet to thank them. Rebecca's fingers brushed his arm.

"They know," she said. He looked down into her eyes. "Even if they don't speak English. Even if you don't tell them a thing about who you are or what you're doing. It shows on your face exactly the kind of man you are and exactly how you feel."

There was an odd lump building in the back of his throat and for a moment he had trouble swallowing. *And what feelings does she see in my eyes when she looks in my face?*

"Just like I'm sure you know the difference you've made in the life of people you've rescued," she added, "even when you don't know the whole story or what happens to them next."

True enough. Like the young, frightened woman he'd extracted from Black Talon's grip months ago. In her early twenties, with hair the color of corn silk, he'd never learned her real name or what had happened to her once she'd reached Canada, but he'd never doubted the difference he'd made in her life.

He'd just never thought of it that way before.

They kept walking down the thin dirt track as it cut back and forth through the woods. Her footsteps moved every bit as silently as his. His ears strained for the sound of danger ahead but heard nothing but the rustle of wind in the trees. The ground sloped steeply beneath them.

The dirt road turned hard to the right. But a path of broken trees and tire tracks continued straight down the hill ahead of them. It seemed someone had driven the truck off the road and straight through the trees. And not willingly, judging by the spent bullets and shell casings littering the ground.

They made their way down the hill without

speaking. Finally, he could see a break in the trees ahead. There was the faint sound of water lapping and insects humming.

Nothing that sounded human.

He stopped walking and held his arm out in front of her.

"Hold up," he whispered. "Let me go ahead, okay? Keep me in your line of sight if you can. Stay behind me but don't come out of the trees until I give you the all clear. If hostiles attack and you hear major weapon fire, make it back to the highway and hide near the spot Jacques dropped us off. I'll come find you."

He half expected her to argue or at least ask questions. Instead, she stood on her tiptoes. Her mouth brushed his ear.

"Okay," she whispered.

He stepped through the woods. The trees parted. A huge, abandoned granite quarry cut deep into the ground, filled with dark green water. The camper was parked near the edge of the quarry lake. Bullet holes riddled the aluminum siding. The camper door hung open on its hinges. Glass and spent bullet casings littered the ground. He couldn't see the truck.

He crept forward, his hands unconsciously clenching for the weapon he didn't have. Inside the camper, he found boxes torn open, their contents strewn. Plastic dishes spilled from cupboards. Computer equipment lay smashed on the floor.

He stepped back and crossed around to the other side of the camper.

Then he saw her truck.

It was submerged and sinking nose first into the quarry, with only the tailgate still peaking above the water's edge.

His bag. His phone. Her laptop containing whatever it was Seth had stolen.

Were they all still in the cab of her truck, now sinking underwater?

SEVEN

Zack stared at the truck. The water was so murky it was hard to tell how deep the quarry was. For a moment he hoped the reason the truck hadn't sunk any farther was that the front bumper was now wedged into the bottom of the lake. But then he saw the thin, taught, knee-high metal cable that connected the wrecked camper to the sinking truck.

So the camper had been detached from the truck's trailer hitch, presumably to stop it from sinking into the water after the truck. Then someone had reattached it using the winch cable on the back of the truck. Had they been hoping to use the winch to pull the submerged truck back up onto the shore? If so, it hadn't worked. The winch motor wasn't turning, but he could hear the faint metallic sound of it straining to pull. The camper creaked slightly.

Whoever was behind this wreck was nowhere to be seen.

He waved a hand toward the tree line. Rebecca was by his side in seconds. He watched as her gaze ran from her camper to the remains of her truck. Then her hands slid over her face.

"I'm sorry, Becs. If we don't detach the winch from the camper, the weight of the truck is going to pull the camper under. But I don't know how deep the quarry lake is. So I need to swim down to the truck and try to retrieve the laptop from the glove compartment before I detach it."

"Is the camper clear?" she asked.

"Tossed, but empty. Can't tell if anything's stolen."

She stared at the truck for a long moment. He braced himself, expecting her to start crying or even rush into his arms. Instead, she turned on her heels and ran for the camper.

"My laptop case is shatterproof and waterproof," she said. "Really heavy-duty. So hopefully whatever it was you downloaded onto it can still be recovered. Just give me a second to change into my scuba gear and then I'll dive down for it."

The camper inched closer to the shore.

"No, the truck's unstable." He followed her. "The cable could snap. The truck could flip with you inside it. Or the camper could get dragged down and crush you. It'll be much safer if you stay here and I dive down."

She didn't even turn. "Don't forget there's a combination lock on the glove compartment. I'm going to be a lot faster unlocking it than you. The combination's my birthday. I've done it a hundred times."

"But never underwater, in the freezing cold, in a submerged truck," he argued. "Besides, you could get down there and discover someone has just smashed it open. And I still remember your birthday."

She paused at the camper door and turned back.

"Okay, but if someone rushes out of those trees and starts shooting while one of us is underwater, it's better you're the one who's up here having our back."

She hopped up into the camper.

"But you're hardly a strong enough swimmer, are you?" His hands rose in frustration. "Remember that time Seth tossed you in the pool at the martial arts team barbecue? You flailed and panicked and shrieked like a nut. Until I dropped my plate of food on the deck and jumped in after you and dragged you back to the shallow end. The water wasn't even that deep." Then Seth had picked up Zack's food and thrown it in at them, while they'd both been there flopping around in the water, fully clothed, while everyone else laughed. "I appreciate your enthusiasm, but flailing is the very last thing we need right now. Just the slightest touch could cause that truck to sink."

The color drained from her face.

"Wow, I can't believe you brought that up, or would use that day against me." She turned away from him, but he could see that her shoulders were shaking.

Okay, that was probably not how he should've phrased it.

"Look, I'm sorry, that might've been out of line, but—"

"You think I don't remember that day or how humiliated I was?" She spun back. He opened his mouth, but she didn't let him get a word in edgewise. "I'll have you know that six months before then I'd been on holiday with my family in Cozumel, learning to scuba dive in the hotel pool, when Seth had snuck up behind me and switched off my oxygen tank. He said he'd done it to teach me 'buddy breathing.' All I'd known was that I suddenly couldn't breathe. At all. I'd been petrified and spent the rest of the holiday hanging on land with my mom, while he was out on the water with the General. That barbecue you remember was my first time near water since then. So yeah, I had a panic attack in a swimming pool in front of you, when I was *sixteen years old.*

"Now, I'm scuba certified. Now, I have more than one wet suit, plus scuba gear in my camper from some preliminary underwater shoots I've done. It won't fit you. Also, considering I'm about half your size, if the truck is sinking, we need the least amount of weight added to it as is possible." She ran both hands through her hair. "You knew who I was as a teenager, Zack. Don't presume to have any idea who I am now."

Thunder rumbled in the distance. Dark clouds were building overhead, blocking out the setting sun. Seconds ticked by. The camper crept closer to the water.

"You're right," he said, "I don't know who you are now and I was wrong to jump to conclusions." Just like she'd only known the infatuated oaf who'd wrapped his arm around her waist, and huffed and puffed his way with her to the shallow end. She'd never known the man who'd once escaped the trunk of a sinking SUV with two panicked foreign aid workers. "It makes the most sense to have the person with the most tactical experience watching the shore and the person who's most familiar with the truck searching it. But if that truck starts to sink, I'm coming in after you. My top priority is keeping you safe. Got it?"

She nodded. "Yes and thank you."

She disappeared into the camper. The door swung shut behind her. For a second he thought it was too damaged to close. But she yanked it so hard the latch finally clicked.

Zack could've kicked himself for bringing up the swimming-pool story. He couldn't imagine how bad he'd feel if she'd brought up some embarrassing story from his past to win an argument. It had been hours since he'd stopped her from getting in the Black Talons' van. Yet she hadn't once brought up how overweight and awkward he used to be. Then again, she'd hardly been the type to comment on it back then, either.

He paced the ground. His eyes first ran over the bullet holes in the side of the camper, then the spent shell casings, scuffed footprints and the glass on the ground, trying to piece together the clues around him and reconstruct what had happened. He ran one hand over his head.

Come on, man, he lectured himself like a new recruit. *Like Rebecca said, solving puzzles used to be your specialty. Put it together. What can you see? What do you know?*

He knew that Seth had stolen Rebecca's

truck and camper. Then Seth, or someone else, had driven it through the woods at a breakneck speed along a narrow dirt track, before swerving off the road and driving straight down through the woods. The truck had ended up in the quarry. The camper had probably been saved from the same fate by being detached from the trailer hitch after the truck went in. Only someone had then attached the camper to a winch on the back of the truck, probably in an attempt to keep the truck from sinking. The direction and size of the bullet holes in the camper implied they were fired on while the vehicle was moving, as opposed to after it crashed.

That was the extent of what he could figure out by sight alone, and even then it involved far more guesswork to fill in the gaps than he was comfortable with.

Then he mentally ran down the list of questions he still didn't have answers for.

Like, had Seth been driving the truck when it crashed, or had it been someone else? Either way, where was Seth now?

Had anyone realized that the computer program he'd had on the memory stick was now on Rebecca's laptop? Was the laptop still in the truck? If so, had the laptop's waterproof case even survived the impact?

How was Black Talon involved in this? How had a female Black Talon operative infiltrated the provincial police? How had she recruited Seth to steal whatever it was he'd stolen from a government facility? Had she then been murdered by Seth or by someone else?

What could possibly prompt Seth Miles, the only son of General Arthur Miles, decorated military hero, to turn traitor and steal something from his own government?

And what had Seth even stolen?

He raised his eyes to the sky as he directed his last question to the Lord as a prayer.

And Lord, how can I catch a traitor, stop Black Talon and protect Rebecca, when just being near her is threatening to unlock parts of my heart I thought I'd shut down for good?

He heard the camper door swing open. He turned.

"I'm afraid I've got some more bad news." Rebecca stood in the doorway in a sleeveless "shorty" wet suit with pant legs that stopped just above her knees. Less coverage than what she'd probably want for a dive into a quarry that deep. Her hand held just a swim mask and flippers. "Some of my scuba gear is missing."

"I did a complete inventory of the big stuff," Rebecca said. "Well, as much as I could. I don't have much that's worth stealing. They definitely tossed the place, and they might've grabbed some food from the cupboard and I wouldn't necessarily notice. But the computer and videography equipment is all still there. The only thing really missing is some scuba gear."

She hopped out of the camper and started toward the lake, barefoot, with her snorkeling mask and flippers in one hand. The ground was cold beneath her soles but that was nothing compared to what the water would be like. Anxiety over what was happening to her life was building painfully in her chest. But she ignored both the devastation of the camper behind her and the wrecked truck in the water ahead, and focused on just taking one step in front of the other.

Her camper and truck had been her entire life. Not just her home and her business—her freedom and her security, too. But she wasn't going to let herself break down and cry. She was going to stay strong. It was bad enough Zack apparently still thought of her as the teenager she used to be. She wasn't about to fall apart in front of him, too.

"But your scuba gear is missing," Zack said. He followed her down to the water.

"Yup. My full-body wet suit is gone, along

with my oxygen tank. I guess someone's already tried to dive down to the truck. Hopefully they didn't find the laptop." She bent down and pulled on her flippers. "Looks like I'm going to have to hold my breath. Fortunately, I've got pretty good lungs."

"But we don't know who stole your gear or where they are now," Zack said.

There was that edge of warning to his voice again. The one that sent shivers down her spine. The sun sat low in the sky. Red-tinged clouds reflected on the surface of the water. She pulled the mask on so hard she felt the elastic snap against her skin and stepped in water up to her ankles. There was a narrow ledge of rock just under the surface, slippery with algae. Beyond that, she'd have to jump.

"Hang on," Zack said. "Maybe I should do it."

"Maybe," she said. "But you should also be up here on land, planning our way out of this and having our back in case whoever tried to attack us comes back. Sadly, there's only one of you and the only backup you've got right now is me."

She took a deep breath, leaped out into the lake and slid beneath the surface. Even with the wet suit protecting her core, the water was so cold it was hard to breathe. Thick, wet tendrils of seaweed curled up around her body. A wall of gray-green water swam before her eyes. The sound of her own breath filled her ears. Then the cab of her truck loomed before her, a dark, ghostly shape suspended in the darkness.

The quarry was so deep she couldn't even see the ground. The truck hadn't sunk to the bottom. Rather it was suspended, between the surface of the water above and the murky depths below, held in place by the cable connecting it to the camper.

Her lungs ached, demanding that it was time to come up for air. But instead, she focused on the truck. Her limbs propelled her toward the driver's-side door. The window was a mess of shattered glass. She reached for the door handle and pulled. The door swung open slowly.

She grabbed her lips to keep from gasping.

There was a man buckled into the driver's seat.

A gray jumpsuit billowed around his body as if trying to pull him through the seat belt. A thin stream of blood floated from the side of his head. Huge hands still gripped the steering wheel. Ivan, the Black Talon mercenary who'd held a gun to her head and forced her into the van, was now dead in the front seat of her truck.

Fear flooded her limbs and for a moment

the heaviness of the shock she felt threatened to pull her downward. She grabbed the door to steady herself. The truck lurched and then dropped another few feet. She flung her body backward in the water and barely avoiding being dragged down with it.

She spun back and swam upward. Sunlight flashed on the surface above her. Her lungs begged for air. Her chest ached suddenly for the strength of Zack's arms encircling her and the comfort of his hand on the back of her head, as he told her it was all going to be okay.

Her body broke through the surface. She gasped, as air filled her lungs.

"What happened?" Zack shouted. The camper was now teetering close to the water's edge. Zack's arms were braced against it, using his own strength to keep the camper from falling into the water. "The truck just suddenly sank like stone!"

There's a body in the truck, Zack! There's a dead body in my truck!

The words screamed through her mind, but her depleted lungs could barely make a sound. Her hands and feet scrambled for the feel of solid ground beneath them.

"Was the laptop still there?" His questions flew at her rapid-fire, with the precision of a military sergeant frustrated from watching a mission falling apart around him. "How about my bag? Did you get it at least? Did you get any sense of how deep the water goes?"

She shook her head and gasped for breath.

"Well, this was a mistake." He rolled his eyes toward the setting sun. "I can't dive down now or the camper might go under. You're not strong enough to keep the camper from falling into the water and I can't unhitch the cable. I tried but it's under too much strain. I'm going to need some tool to either cut the cable or break the camper hitch off altogether. But if you can't get the laptop from the truck, either—"

He bit the end of his sentence back without finishing it and instead just shook his head in frustration.

She felt useless. As though he thought she was nothing but some frightened waste of space.

A liability.

"I never should've put you in this position," he said. "You're hardly trained for any of this. Just swim back to shore and I'll figure out what we're going to do from here."

Rebecca took a deep breath and felt the comfort of air filling her lungs. Then she dived down again.

She could hear the distorted sound of Zack

shouting echo above the water. She didn't stop. She didn't need to hear what he was saying. The look on his face had been clear. Zack thought she was some awkward klutz who'd flailed around foolishly, made the truck sink and cost him their only chance at recovering the stolen material.

Zack and Seth might be fighting on different sides of a battle, but their opinions of her seemed to be the same. She was going to prove them both wrong.

The swim was deeper this time. The pain in her lungs was sharper. But her focus was clearer. Her arms and legs propelled her swiftly down to the truck and around to the passenger side. Broken glass ringed the hole where the shattered windshield had been. She grabbed the passenger door handle. The truck dropped another foot, yanking the handle from her hand. She tried again. The door was stuck.

Rebecca held tight to the door frame as the sinking truck pulled her down toward the bottom of the quarry. She slid around over the hood and swam through the open windshield. Ivan's dead face loomed toward her. She forced her eyes away. The handle of Zack's bag floated up from under the seat. She looped it around her wrist. Then her hands grabbed the glove compartment and she punched in the code, praying it would open.

It fell open. Her laptop slid out still in its case. *Thank You, God.* She grabbed it with the other hand and swam upward. Her lungs were screaming so hard for oxygen now that she had to press her lips together to keep them from parting. Lights swam before her eyes.

Just two more seconds. Two more kicks.

Then it would all be over. Then she'd be able to breathe again.

A figure in a black wet suit loomed above her.

Like a shark encircling its prey.

Blocking her way to the surface.

EIGHT

She was going to drown.

That was the first thought that filled her mind.

The figure in the black wet suit turned. He swam at her.

Seth's blue eyes focused on hers through her stolen scuba mask.

Years of getting over her fear of drowning and her stepbrother was actually going to try to drown her.

He grabbed her arm. She struck back hard, hitting him squarely in the jaw, trying to knock the breathing apparatus from his face. Seth let go. She kicked back hard, her feet pushing off against his body as she swam hard for the surface. The bag dragged her down. The laptop was slipping from her fingers. She shoved it into the shoulder bag praying it wouldn't fall out.

Her body broke through the surface.

"Zack!" she gasped. "Help!"

But she'd barely managed a breath when she felt the squeeze of Seth's hand clamp her ankle. Seth yanked her back under. Bubbles filled her eyes. Water filled her lungs. She felt herself dropping. Her body tumbled down into the cold, dark depths. Seth's arm was around her neck. He forced something to her mouth.

Oxygen.

Air filled her lungs. His eyes met hers through his swim mask. Seth had given her his oxygen. She held it to her mouth, and they stayed there, for a long moment, locked together by a single tank of oxygen, as their bodies sank down to the depths, beside the sinking truck.

Then with one hand, Seth grabbed the strap. With the other, he grabbed the breathing apparatus.

Give me the bag. She could read the words in his pale blue eyes. *The oxygen or the bag. You choose.* She took a deep breath. Seth yanked hard on the bag. *Just let go, Rebecca. Give up. Quit fighting. And then this'll all be over.*

The water churned above them. Something was coming toward them, tearing up the water in its path.

Zack!

He grabbed Seth from behind and yanked

him back. Then he leveled a blow on the back of Seth's head, the water moving around them as if they were fighting in slow motion.

Rebecca let go of the oxygen mask and kicked Seth back with every ounce of strength she had left. Seth grabbed the oxygen, gasped a breath and spun toward Zack. His hands locked on Zack's throat. Seth might've gone easy on Rebecca, but she had no doubt that if it came to it, Seth would let Zack drown.

Desperately, her fingers ran through Zack's bag until she felt the cold edge of a utility knife. She yanked it out, grabbed Seth's oxygen line and drove the tip into it. Bubbles filled water as oxygen escaped in a rush around them. She swam for the surface, praying with every stroke that Zack and Seth would both make it up alive.

Four strong kicks and her head burst through the surface. She crawled to shore. The camper was hanging over the edge of the quarry and tilting sharply. She tossed the bag and climbed inside the camper. It shook under her feet.

She dropped to the floor, threw open the hatch under her bed and yanked out an ax. Then she climbed out, braced herself on the ledge and swung. The ax blade screeched against the metal cable. Bubbles rose to the surface of the water. *Please Lord, bring both*

Zack and Seth to the surface alive. She swung again, throwing her full might into the blow. The cable snapped. Sharp wire flew back toward her. The camper broke free. The surface of the water surged as the truck dropped like a stone.

Seth's face broke through the surface of the water. Pale. Ragged. Alone.

Her heart stopped.

"Where's Zack?"

Seth gasped for breath. She leaped down and readied the ax, ready to swing. Hot tears rushed to her eyes.

"Where is Zack? If you've hurt him, I'll—"

Zack rose through the water behind him. Water streamed from his hair and down the lines of his face. His wet T-shirt was plastered down his muscular chest like something carved out of marble. A grim smile turned at the corners of his lips as his eyes met hers.

Her heart lurched as the relief of seeing his face crashed hard against the knowledge of just how deep the pain had been at the thought of losing him.

Zack's not mine. He'll never be mine. But if anything had happened to him, my heart would've shattered.

Zack yanked Seth by the back of the neck and dragged him onto the shore.

"Got the laptop and the bag?" Zack asked.

"Yeah." She stood there, the ax still clutched in her hands, feeling relieved and uncertain as to what to do next, and yet desperate to be in the arms of the man now yanking her stepbrother up toward the camper.

"You sank the truck," Zack said, with a tone she couldn't quite read. He was knelt over Seth. His knee pressed into Seth's back. Zack glanced toward the dark clouds now moving across purple sky. "I hope we got everything out of it that we need, because the oxygen tank's ruined and I don't know if we've got enough light for another dive."

"There was a dead body in the truck, Zack, that's why the truck sank earlier." She could feel her voice rising with the desire to defend herself from Zack's unspoken accusation. "Ivan, the Black Talon thug who tried to kidnap me, was in the driver's seat. That's why I came back up for air. Then I had to cut the cable while you were underwater or we'd have totally lost the camper."

He just nodded like his brain was silently processing the information. Then he said, "My handcuffs are with my jacket, on the ground by the camper. Do you have anything I can tie his legs up with?

"There's packing tape in the camper," she said. "But it's not that great."

"Well, it'll have to do," Zack said. "Just let me get him tied up and then I'll help you push the camper a little farther back onto the shore."

She turned back to the camper.

"Don't do it, Becs!" Seth's voice made her stop. "Please. You can't trust Zack."

"Zack? I can't trust *Zack*?" she repeated, turning back. "You're the one who bullied me through high school. You blew up the rocks I was standing on. You stole my truck and my camper. You practically threatened to drown me."

"Should've known you'd never understand." Seth was looking up at her from the ground, still under Zack's grasp. "I took what I did from that computer because I *thought* it would help save lives. I came to you for your help when everything suddenly went south. And stole your truck because you wouldn't help me. I only blew up the road to keep Zack from getting to you, and if you'd let me we could've shared my oxygen long enough to get away from him together." Disgust filled his voice. "But you're siding with the enemy."

"The enemy? You think Zack is your enemy?" She crouched down until they were eye level. "Zack is the only person I've ever been able to count on to have my back. You're a thief and a murderer."

"I never killed anyone!"

"What about the dead body in my truck?"

"I didn't kill him!"

"Then who did?" Rebecca asked.

He didn't answer. She stood up slowly.

"You think Zack's trustworthy?" Seth asked. "Zack didn't tell you what was going on. He didn't even tell you I was involved. I bet he didn't even tell you there's a warrant out for your arrest? That you're wanted for conspiracy to commit treason and murder? It's all over the news. I'm accused of killing a cop, which means you're accused of helping me kill a cop. You get anywhere near a police station, they'll toss you in jail and throw away the key. And Zack will stand by and let them do it!"

"Don't even try." She almost snorted. "I'm not going to believe you now."

"I'm not lying!" Seth looked up at the man still holding him down in the dirt. "Am I, Zack? Tell her! Tell Rebecca the truth. I'm accused of killing a cop, aren't I? She's accused of being an accomplice. There's a warrant out for her arrest, isn't there? You know full well the moment police spot Rebecca, they're going to draw their guns and handcuff her. If she sticks with you she'll end up behind bars, and you didn't even warn her."

"That's not true, is it, Zack?" Her eyes searched Zack's face.

Zack gritted his teeth. He looked past Rebecca into the trees.

"It appears the woman wasn't a real cop," he said, finally. "And yes, she did pass away from her injuries."

Seth tried to twist his head around to face him. "Who was she?"

"I don't know."

"How long had she been in Canada?" Seth asked. "Please, just tell me that?"

Zack shook his head as if there was water in his ears. "I don't see why that matters. But my understanding is that she'd been with the police force for a couple of years, and she was not who she'd claimed to be."

The relief on Seth's face was palpable.

But Rebecca didn't get what he had to be relieved about. "Is this your way of dancing around the fact that she might've been a Black Talon criminal hidden in the Ontario Provincial Police?"

"I can't discount the possibility," Zack said.

"You knew there was a warrant issued for my *arrest*?"

"I did."

"And didn't tell me?"

Thunder rumbled in the distance.

"I didn't tell you." Zack's facial expression didn't even flicker. "I did my job."

Zack raised his knuckles toward the broken camper door, hesitated and then knocked.

"Come in."

He opened the door. Rebecca was standing with her back to him in the shambles of her camper. She gripped the thin counter with both hands. She'd changed out of her wet suit into a pair of jeans and an oversize sweatshirt. But even through the thick folds of fabric he could see her arms were shaking. He could see the last red rays of the setting sun filtering through the trees in the window ahead of him, but faint rain now fell off the camper's canopy behind him, as if they were caught in a tiny sliver of space in the unsettled weather patterns.

Rebecca's laptop lay open on the tiny table showing the same black screen with red Cyrillic letters that it had when he'd shut it down. The case was cracked but had managed to keep her laptop safe and dry. Not that they were any closer to finding out the password. Seth now sat on the ground in front of the camper, with his hands cuffed behind his back and his legs bound by packing tape at his ankles. He'd refused to speak to Zack ever since Rebecca had stormed into the camper. Not a word. Not even so much as a grunt. And as much as Seth was pulling Zack's patience to the limits, Zack knew he wasn't authorized to interrogate Seth. Nor was he about to lay a hand on him.

But maybe Rebecca would have better results in getting answers from him. Certainly Seth had seemed eager to talk, to have Rebecca on his side. Only it seemed Rebecca didn't feel much like talking to Zack right now, either. The thirty-eight year-old ran his hand through his prematurely graying hair. His phone was still missing and likely lost to the quarry. Rebecca's phone had been broken in the rock slide. When he'd patted Seth down, he'd found nothing on him but his wallet. Looked like their only hope now was to walk Seth back to the road and flag a vehicle down for help. Either that or he could leave Seth here with Rebecca and head back by himself.

Neither option appealed to him much.

"How's it going?" Zack's hand hovered over her back, waiting for a signal it was okay to touch her. After she'd discovered he'd known about the warrant for her arrest, she'd barely spoken to him besides getting him the packing tape.

"Hey, any chance of some dinner out here?"

Seth called from outside the door. "Maybe some of that horrible bean soup you make? Some of us are hungry."

Rebecca turned around. She looked down at Zack's hand still outstretched in front of her. He slid it into his pocket.

"Are you hungry?" she asked. "I'm thinking you haven't eaten in hours."

He shrugged. "I'm not particularly hungry. But I could eat."

She turned toward the cupboards, crouched down and pulled out a large silver tin.

"You told me once that you were always hungry," she said.

"No, I was always sad," he said. "I just hadn't figured out how to tell the difference between hungry and sad back then."

She opened the lid and dumped a mixture of dried vegetables, beans, lentils and herbs into a pot. Then poured in some bottled water and stirred.

"Eventually, I replaced food with exercise," he added. "After you and I went our separate ways, I exercised way too much at first. Like five or six hours a day. Finally I got better at finding balance."

She pulled a tiny gas burner out from under the sink, set it on the counter and lit the flame. Then she set the pot on top.

"You'd lost a good chunk of weight in the months before the sports banquet," she said after a long moment. "Was that the reason why?"

He paused, wondering how to answer the question.

"No," he said. "It was because hanging with you so much made me really happy."

She didn't answer. The glimmer of sun disappeared outside. She switched on a battery lamp, then reached up and attached it to a hook above his head. The rain fell harder. The soup bubbled. The camper felt crowded. As though it was filled to the brim with questions neither of them knew how to ask and words neither of them were ready to say.

"We should eat," Zack said finally. "Then we should take turns napping, to keep our strength up. I'm only going to need about fifteen minutes, but you should have at least an hour. After that we're going to have to find a way to signal for help. It might be best if we all head back to the main road, but to be honest I don't want to take action until I've really thought it through."

"I'm going to be arrested by the first cop we see, aren't I?" She leaned back against the counter. "I'm going to be handcuffed and carted away with Seth, and we'll have no way of knowing if the person arresting me is a real cop or some Black Talon criminal."

"That's not going to happen. I promise. I won't let it." In one step, Zack had crossed the camper. He pulled her into his arms and she let him. He felt her body shaking as he held her tightly to his chest. Then he brushed the fingers of one hand against her chin, and tilted her head until she looked up at him.

"Listen to me," he said. "I won't let anybody I don't trust take you anywhere. And I will never let anyone hurt you. Ever. I've always been there for you and I'm always going to be there for you. I promise."

"You can't promise that, because that's not true." She looked up into his face, and he could see both strength and pain battling inside her eyes. "You're not going to be there when I need you, Zack. Just like you disappeared from my life the last time, when you were the one person I was counting on to help hold me together. You weren't there for me when my mother died, and I was left with nothing but this camper and this land, so I had to drop out of university and rebuild my life from the ground up. You're not going to be there for me in two days when you need to report back to base for deployment. You're not going to be there for me next week, next month, next year, when you're off getting shot at and saving lives wherever in the world you are."

The pot bubbled over. He let go. She turned back to the counter, lowered the heat and stirred.

"I'm sorry if that sounds harsh," she added. "Because I know you're a really good guy and I believe you mean what you're saying. But I'm nothing but a short-term mission here, Zack, and I know it. At the end of the day, I have to save myself, and the more secrets you keep from me, the more you're just putting my life in danger."

He stepped back and stared at her shoulders. He wanted to reach out and hug her again. To hold her. To promise that he'd always be there and that he'd never leave. But he couldn't. So instead, he bent down and started picking up random things off the floor—clothes, books, dishes, equipment—and piling them on a shelf beside her narrow bunk.

A glint of gold caught his eye. He reached for it.

It was her martial arts trophy. His eyes ran over the inscription.

"They had a medal for you that night, too, you know," she said. She looked down at the trophy in his hands. "Which you would've known if you'd showed up to the banquet. I meant to tell you. But I was too hurt at first, and then when you told me you'd joined the military, I was so surprised I forgot."

"What did it say?"

"Biggest Heart." She turned back and unclipped the three plastic mugs that still hung attached to hooks over the tiny sink and poured soup into each of them in turn. "Fitting, right? You had the biggest heart of anyone I knew, back then."

There was this edge to her voice, as if she thought there was nothing left in his rib cage now but dust and ashes.

"I still have a heart, Rebecca," he said gruffly. "And it's as big as it ever was. I just got a whole lot better at controlling it."

"Because you decided to turn it off." She said it lightly, and somehow the fact that she could make it sound as though it was nothing irked him even more than if she'd sounded serious.

"No, because somebody broke it."

Thunder crashed. The rain poured hard around them, beating down against the ground. Outside, he could hear Seth complaining he was getting wet. But inside, it was as if the walls had shrunk. The beat of his own heart filled his ears. The mugs shook in Rebecca's hands.

"Broke your heart?" She stepped closer. Her

voice dropped to a whisper. "Who broke your heart, Zack?"

You did, Rebecca. You did on the night of the sports banquet. How can you not know that?

"It doesn't matter." He looked up to the rain pounding on the skylight above their heads. "I probably needed to have my heart broken. It helped me get where I needed to be. Helped me focus. Helped me train. Helped me save countless lives. Helped me learn how to engage my brain, calm down and be rational. Instead of charging off after every surge of emotion I was feeling, like—"

Like I did today. Like when I hopped on my motorcycle and flew up the highway to see you when I saw your brother's face on the television screen.

The air in the camper grew darker. Her breath brushed up against his neck.

"Like I ran through the pouring rain in just my jeans and a T-shirt, without an umbrella or even a jacket, in a torrential downpour, the night you got this trophy." He tossed it onto the bunk. "The storm was so bad that night I could see motorcycles and garbage cans getting washed down the streets of the base. But there I was, plowing on through the storm, like some foolish, unbridled, reckless kid, five seconds after hitting the send button on my online military application, just to tell you I had."

And the moment he'd gotten there, and seen the look of utter disgust on her face, he'd known there was no way she could ever love a man like him.

"Hey!" Seth's voice floated through the crack in the partially open door. "I'm drowning out here. Could someone bring me a bath towel? A paper towel? Anything?"

Zack grabbed the largest of the three mugs from Rebecca's hands and tossed it back, drinking it straight down without even pausing for breath. Hot soup stung his throat. He dropped the empty mug in the sink.

"You should go talk to Seth." Zack sat down on the bunk. "Maybe he'll tell you something useful, like the password he's locked your computer with or how a dead Black Talon ended up in your truck. You might be our best chance to get answers out of him. I'm going to take a quick nap. Then I'll figure out our next move."

Zack set the alarm on his watch for fifteen minutes. Rebecca hesitated.

"Look," he added, "this might be the last chance you ever get to have a conversation with him that doesn't involve talking through a sheet of Plexiglas. Besides, he really sounds like he wants soup. I could use some quiet, to think our way out of this."

Zack leaned back on the foam mattress and closed his eyes. He heard her feet creek on the camper floor. The door swung open then shut. He pressed his hands into his eyes.

If he'd gotten so good at controlling his wayward heart, then what was this fierce and foolish beat he could feel thudding like a fist in his chest right now?

Lord, why is my heart still so drawn to a woman who can never be mine? How do I get us all out of here alive?

He lay down on her bunk and stared at the ceiling.

Please Lord, help her get the truth out of Seth. It might not solve all our problems, but it'll definitely make life easier if he stops fighting us.

His head was spinning. His body felt weak. His stomach felt nauseous. He turned over and reached to grab a book out of the shelf to his right, feeling for a Bible.

Instead, the mustached grin of General Arthur Miles stared back at him from the cover of his autobiography.

His friends in the unit always liked to tease him that if only he'd been smart enough to marry the General's stepdaughter, he'd be company quartermaster sergeant by now. Not that he'd ever wanted to do a job other than the one he was doing now. But now, something about the whole premise of the joke gave him pause. What if he'd stayed with Rebecca and had realized that admiring a man's military record wasn't the same as liking the person behind the hero's mask? He'd never once stopped to consider what would've happened to his career if he hadn't liked how the General treated Rebecca or her mother. Or worse yet, if the General had disliked him.

While he deeply disliked the idea of someone creating an anonymous blog to attack the man, he had to admit that going up against a man of that stature could seriously hamper a soldier's opportunity for advancement or hurt a promising career.

Or even get him court-martialed.

He opened the book at random. The words swam on the page.

Nausea swept over him again. For a long, agonizing moment it felt as if the bunk was spinning. Then unconsciousness hit him like a brick.

NINE

Rebecca stood outside the camper and looked down at her stepbrother.

Seth was huddled pitifully in a dry patch of dirt that was rapidly growing smaller with the encroaching rain. He glanced at the plastic mugs, then turned his back toward her so that she could see the handcuffs. "I'm supposed to drink that how exactly?"

She sat down on the thin camper step. "Nice try, but I'm not about to free your hands."

She set one mug beside her, and held the other one up to his mouth. He made a half-hearted show of trying to take a sip without actually drinking anything. She set the mug back down and leaned against the side of the camper archway. Seth stared out at the rain with an expression that was pathetic, wounded and self-righteous all at once. "I can't believe you thought I'd kill someone. I didn't. I downloaded something from a computer. That's all."

And blew up the road, threatened her life and attacked Zack more than once.

"I'll ask you again, why is there a dead body in the cab of my truck?"

Seth shrugged.

"That man put a gun to my head," she said. "That man tried to kidnap me. I know he's a member of some organized crime ring from the former Soviet Union called Black Talon. So, I'll ask my question again." She raised her voice and repeated herself, slowly dragging out the words one syllable at a time. "Why is there a dead body in my truck?"

"I don't know what's going on exactly." Seth turned and looked at her. "I'd never heard of Black Talon before."

"Then what were you doing meeting a Black Talon operative in a park after you stole that computer program?"

Seth ignored the question. "Ivan and his buddy Dmitry in the red van kidnapped me. They drove off into the woods and I figured I was going to die. I figured that was it for me. Especially as I had no clue what had happened to the program they wanted or that Zack had downloaded it onto your laptop. I was just trying to run at that point. Anyway, then some other vehicle, big black one, starts firing at us. More people with bird tattoos shooting at the people with bird tattoos who'd just kidnapped me. Then there was swerving and shouting and glass shattering and trees smacking against us. Dmitry jumps out. I realize Ivan's dead. Then we crash into the quarry and the truck starts sinking. So, I swim to shore and hide. Dmitry detaches the camper from the truck and tears it up, looking for the computer program. He leaves. I search the camper and when I can't find it realize I should've searched the truck, so I attach your camper to the truck with the winch and try to pull it up. Doesn't work. I grab scuba gear. I hear someone's coming, so I hide underwater. That's where you come in. End of story."

There was a finality to Seth's voice that implied he would've crossed his arms if he was able.

"So, you just happened to end up in the middle of some kind of war between two factions of an Eastern European criminal syndicate who both want what you've got?"

"Looks like it," Seth said. "Again, I don't care whether you believe me or not. But I lifted something from a government computer for altruistic reasons. I was trying to help someone. I was trying to right a wrong. Then I finally meet the person I thought sent me to find the program, and she's shot in front of me. I come running to you, because I'm at my wit's end about what to do, and you're the only one who might even understand—"

"Why? Why would I possibly understand?"

Again, he ignored her question.

"And I end up trapped between competing interests who both want something I have in my possession." He tilted his head back, leaned back against the camper and stared up at the canopy above him. "I never imagined anyone would issue a warrant for your arrest. I did use some of your old email addresses and social media accounts to do some stuff online, when I was trying to talk to my contact without creating a trail. But no one should've seen that. Even if they did, I hacked you. You shouldn't get arrested over something like that."

Zack's watch alarm went off. Guess his fifteen minute cat nap had ended. She pushed the door open a crack, expecting to see Zack sitting up. Instead Zack was lying on the bunk on his back, with his eyes closed and the General's autobiography lying on his chest as though he'd passed out while reading it. His watch alarm beeped for a full minute, then stopped.

"Can't crack your laptop yet, can you?" Seth's voice dragged her attention back outside. "Neither can I. The only person I thought had the password is the same person who I thought I was meeting, and until recently I thought that person was dead. But now that I know she's not dead, that changes everything." And here he actually grinned.

"I really want to let you in," he went on. "Believe me, I do. I just can't trust military boy in there. This secret is too huge. If he knew what I knew he'd probably just suppress it and bury it out of some perverse sense of duty. But you untie me, we get rid of him, and I'll tell you everything you want to know."

"What's the matter with you?" She picked up the mug that she hadn't offered to Seth and took a sip. "When we were kids I thought you hated Zack because he was overweight and too emotionally sensitive. Now, he's strong and successful. I thought he'd be like your ideal of what a man should be. He's everything you used to want to be."

Zack was a lot closer to being like the man whose autobiography now rested on his chest than either Seth or Rebecca would ever be.

"You wouldn't get it," Seth said bitterly.

"You keep saying that. Of course I wouldn't get it! The person with the answers can't stop spouting lies at me. What's your problem with Zack now? Are you jealous that he's succeeding in the military, following in the General's footsteps? Worried that the General's disappointed you didn't turn out to be more like Zack?"

"Stop calling him the General!" Seth shouted, so loudly and angrily his voice seemed to clash with the pounding rain. "It sounds like you think he's important. His name is Arthur Miles. My father. Your father. And he's not a hero. He's just some guy who was good at getting people to do whatever he wanted them to do!"

"So, you believe he cheated on our mothers." She took a deep swig of soup to keep her jaw from dropping. "You blame him for the fact your mother left."

"My mother didn't just leave. She vanished from my life!" Seth's voice was so upset, he almost sounded hysterical. "You think I'm sulky because my father was a bad husband? Wake up, Becs! I was trying to protect my sister. He sent *criminals* after my sister!"

Her head ached, with a throbbing pain that somehow seemed to spread into her eye sockets. She yawned. "Your father sent Black Talon operatives after me?"

"No." Seth's face went pale. "Of course, he didn't."

"But you just said he did. Were you trying to protect me from your father?"

Seth clamped his mouth shut.

"I didn't know what I was saying," Seth said

finally, in a tone that seemed to land somewhere being lying and truth. "That's not what I meant. Obviously, I'm too upset what with being kidnapped by gangsters and then held prisoner by my own stepsister to know what I'm saying."

Seth was talking gibberish. As if he was trying to dance in circles around topics of conversation, throwing his words out like sucker punches without landing any of them.

"What I meant to say is that I was trying to protect you from Zack," he said. "Back in the day, it was obvious Zack had a huge, major puppy-dog crush on my only sister, even though he wasn't good enough for you. So, I stepped up and showed you what kind of guy he really was. Never imagined you'd go running back to him now."

"When did you step up and show me what kind of guy Zack actually was?" she asked.

No answer. Her throat stung. She took another sip of soup.

"You're not making any sense," she added. "You can't even stay on one topic for more than a second. If you want to tell me something, just be straight with me and tell me."

But Seth had gone silent again. Behind her she could hear Zack snoring softly.

She finished her soup. The rain fell. The

wind shook the trees. The night grew darker. Seth tilted his head back and sang snippets of some old show tunes that she vaguely recognized, stringing them together in a random melody.

She ignored him. After a while, he went silent.

"You hate me," Seth said quietly.

It wasn't a question, just a statement. She looked down at her huddled stepbrother. His blond hair was wet and plastered over his forehead like a teenager's. But the lines around his pained eyes made him look older, tired and weary.

Lord, she prayed, *I've tried so many times to forgive him. And now... It's like my heart doesn't even begin to know how to start.*

"I don't want to hate you," she said. "But maybe I wanted to at first. I didn't even know how my mother knew General Miles. Suddenly they're married and I get this bombastic, arrogant brother taking up so much space and making so much noise in my house. It was hard. You weren't the easiest person to live with."

"Ouch." There was a plainness to the one-syllable word that made her pause.

She'd expected a pithy comeback or insult, something designed to remind her that he'd always been the popular golden child who'd had friends and sports, who was voted onto student council and played bass guitar in a band. He'd even missed the chance to remind his gangly, clumsy, socially awkward stepsister that she was nothing but a loser.

"I'm being honest." She drained her cup and set it down in the dirt. "It's not entirely your fault. My mom's health problems didn't help. You'd just lost your mother and here your father was suddenly remarried. The General was hardly there for any of us. I just wish we'd stuck together instead of you always pushing me away. Brothers and sisters should stick together. At least that's what you said before you stole my truck."

She yawned again. Her brain felt fuzzy at the edges, as if it had suddenly hit her how tired she was, and she needed to sleep immediately.

"I loved you and hated you and admired you and was jealous of you." Words kept flowing from her mouth, as if she didn't know how to stop them. "Right now, mostly I'm ashamed of you. Because you were always so smart, so clever and so strong. You could've done anything in your life. Instead you treated everyone around you like garbage when we were teenagers, and then in the end you did less than nothing with your life. You became a criminal. And so, yeah, I wish you'd never become a part of my family, because you're a terrible excuse for a brother."

Seth winced as if she'd just slapped him. Pain filled his eyes. She clasped a hand over her mouth.

"I'm sorry. I don't know why I just said that." Her head felt dizzy. Darkness filled the skies above. She opened her mouth to speak, but her words were swallowed up in a yawn.

"Ever heard of a girl named Maria?" Seth asked.

"No..." Her brain was spinning too fast now to make sense of his words.

"Think, Rebecca! Have you ever heard anyone mention the name Maria?"

Maria. Maria in the dead of winter. Maria in the snow, snow, snow...

Seth's show tunes ditty from before was now spinning in her mind. Her head was really throbbing. Her brain screamed at her that she should be listening.

The soup. He'd put something in the soup...

She'd been drugged.

Her head drooped to her chest. Her eyes began to close.

"Listen to me, Rebecca!" Seth was suddenly shouting. His voice was strained. "Pay attention! Please!" She jerked her eyes open. "I created that blog about our father. Me! But I didn't have the information I needed to prove everything I wanted to prove. Needed to prove. But then Maria contacted me and said she could help. She told me there was something on a government computer that would unlock the files I was trying to hack. So I downloaded the file. But I couldn't open it. Then I went to meet her in the park, only it wasn't really Maria, and somebody killed her. So I ran. I came to see you because you were decent, and my sister, and I hoped you could help me."

There were motions in the trees. Figures were approaching. Men in dark clothes.

Her eyes drifted shut again.

"Wake up, Rebecca!" Seth yelled. "Please! You've got to wake up and let me go!"

She needed Zack. Zack would know what to do. Zack would protect her. She turned toward the camper. Her body slipped from the step. She fell into the dirt beside Seth.

"I'm so sorry, Rebecca," Seth was babbling now. "I know I messed up. I was hoping if I tricked you guys into drinking the soup, you'd pass out and I could escape. I promise I never meant to hurt you. Remember the sports banquet? Where you thought that Zack stood you up and you got that trophy?"

Where she thought Zack had stood her up? Of course he'd stood her up. She'd waited for him by the front door for an hour. He hadn't been there.

People were running toward them now. Footsteps were coming closer. She tried to lift her head, but it wouldn't move. She was drifting again, her drugged mind rising to consciousness for fleeting moments only to be pulled back under.

Her head lolled onto Seth's shoulder.

"Remember the trophy!" Seth shouted. "Whatever you do, remember the trophy! Please. No matter what happens next. Remember the trophy!"

Hands grabbed her body. She was lifted. She was helpless. Unable to move her limbs. Unable to fight back.

"Hey God, it's me, Seth," he prayed. "I don't know how this prayer thing works. But my sister needs Your help. Just save her, okay? No matter what happens to me. Don't let them hurt her. Please—"

The sound of Seth screaming filled the air.

But the darkness was so heavy, she couldn't open her eyes.

Rebecca was floating, moving through the air. Voices were talking in a language she couldn't understand. Seth was shouting, but his voice seemed to be coming from a long way away, and her eyes wouldn't open. Then she was lying on something soft. It started moving, rumbling. The ground was shaking underneath her face.

"Rebecca!" Zack shouted. "Rebecca, wake up."

She opened her eyes. She was lying alone on the cot of her camper. Her hands were tied behind her back. Her legs were bound at the ankle. Packing tape covered her mouth. She rubbed her mouth against the bunk vigorously, relief filling her chest as she felt it peel away. Seemed their kidnappers had used the cheap packing tape she'd left on the counter. Unfortunately they'd wound it so many times around her limbs that it would take a good sharp blade to get them free.

She felt around the bunk with her legs. The laptop was gone. The camper rumbled beneath her. Night rushed past the window. They were moving.

"Zack!" Her eyes scanned the camper in the darkness. "Zack, where are you?"

"Down here. On the floor."

She slid her body over to the edge of the bed and looked down, waiting for her eyes to adjust to the darkness. Zack was lying on the camper floor, wedged between the counter and the desk. "Are you okay? Are you hurt?"

"I've been a whole lot better. But I've also been worse." His voice was grim. "We were drugged, and hard. They tied my ankles and wrists. Gagged me, too, but I managed to work that loose. Did you see who did this to us?"

"No. Seth drugged us, but he didn't kidnap us. He seemed genuinely terrified of whoever it was." She prayed that Seth was still alive, wherever he was. "Seth told me that Ivan and Dmitry kidnapped him and then other Black Talon people killed Ivan. He thinks that some members of Black Talon are fighting amongst themselves for whatever he downloaded."

"It's entirely possible."

Her memory was foggy, though, as though someone had come along and tried to erase from her mind everything that had happened after that second sip of soup. He'd said other things. Important things. Something about the woman in the park and show tunes. But she couldn't piece her memories together enough to make sense of them. "Where's Seth?"

"I have no idea," Zack said. "The bigger questions now are where are they taking us and how do we get untied before we get there. When we stop moving, I want to be on my feet and ready to fight." He glanced up at the sky-light. "Or better yet, out of here first."

She looked around for her clock. Five in the morning. The road was rough beneath them. She could hear rocks kicking up underneath the camper. Tree branches smacked against the window. Wherever they were going, it was definitely off-road. "How long have you been awake?"

"About two seconds longer than you," he said. "I'm going to try to find a way to get this tape off. See if you can find anything sharp."

She twisted her wrists behind her back. They were so tight she could barely move.

"Hang on, I've got a thought." She inched to the edge of the bed and started kicking the hard metal edge of one of the brackets she used to convert the cot into the table. The screws had rusted years ago, and the metal had warped and bent over time until it had the unfortunate habit of stabbing her in the shins. She kicked as hard as she could. One end broke free from the wall. She looped the packing tape binding her feet onto the edge of the broken metal and pulled. The tape began to rip. She yanked harder and heard the tape tearing. Then the metal bracket came clear and flew across the floor. "I'm sorry."

"Don't worry." Zack was already sliding his

body toward it. "Just focus on getting yourself free."

She lay on her back and bicycled her legs around and around, pulling at the small tear in the packing tape.

"Got it." Zack's voice floated up from below her. She looked down. He was holding it between his fingers, his hands still taped behind his back. Zack wedged the jagged piece of metal into a small gap between the cupboards then worked it back and forth between his wrists like a knife.

The camper was definitely slowing. The sound beneath the tires sounded wooden. She kicked her legs free and scooted across the bed until she reached the spot where the metal had broken off. She turned her back to it, and following Zack's lead, started rubbing the tape around her wrists against the screws that remained.

"Seth said he'd stolen the program for altruistic reasons," she said. "He'd never heard of Black Talon until they were trying to kill him."

Zack was struggling with his hands. "Well, I wouldn't be so quick to trust Seth."

"When have you ever known me to be quick to trust anybody? I don't trust him. But you asked me to find out what I could and it sounded like whatever he was trying to tell me was really important to him."

Her hands ached. Her shoulders ached. The tape was getting looser. But she could still barely move her hands.

"Okay. I've just about got my hands free," Zack said. "Just about. Just let me get my legs and then I'll get your hands."

There were voices outside. Footsteps.

Zack yanked his hands free and started furiously working on cutting his ankles. Desperately she worked the tape binding her wrists.

There was the metallic clunk of the camper detaching from the vehicle pulling it.

She gave up on her hands and slid her body across the bed, feet raised together, ready to kick whoever opened the door. She could hear Zack praying desperately under his breath. She joined in, her own prayers moving wordlessly over her lips. The voices outside stopped.

There was silence. Then a bump so hard it tossed her off the bed and onto the floor.

Strong arms grabbed her. Zack's body cradled around hers.

Then they were tumbling. Rolling. Airborne.

The camper was falling.

TEN

Zack's arms tightened around Rebecca, and he braced himself around her as he felt his body smash hard into the ceiling of the camper. Then they were flying through the air again. Tossed from ceiling, to walls, to floor as the camper rolled, like Ping-Pong balls in a dryer. Her belongings smacked into him like shrapnel. There was the sound of metal screeching, things breaking. He closed his eyes and bowed his head, feeling her inside his arms.

Lord, we need You now.

There was a shudder and the sound of water crashing around them. The camper stopped rolling. Freezing water roared around them and seeped through the cracks around the windows. The camper turned and twisted beneath them.

He looked up.

The camper had landed on its side in a river. His feet were still bound.

The sky was growing light around them as the sun began to rise. Rebecca slipped from his arms and curled beside him on the floor. "I'm okay. You okay?"

"Yeah."

"Thank God," she prayed.

"Amen."

But the camper was sinking. Water seemed to be seeping in from all directions. The camper spun, tossed by the current. The door hung open above them. He sloshed around in the water, feeling for something sharp to free his legs with. Rebecca tried to stand up, but lost her footing and fell back into the water.

"Untie my hands, please." Even on her knees the water was up to her stomach.

Her hair fell wet and loose around her face. Golden light of the rising sun illuminated her face. Her eyes looked up into his, silently begging him for help. But it wasn't the same desperate, pleading look he'd seen countless times before from people waiting on him to save them and be their hero.

No, Rebecca wasn't begging him for rescue. Instead, she fixed his face with a calm, steady gaze that seemed to say, *Please, Zack, don't let me down.*

"Hang on." His fingers grabbed a kitchen knife. Not as sharp as he'd have liked but far better than nothing. He slid it into the hole he'd already cut in the tape surrounding his feet and started hacking. "We don't have much time and I can't swim out of here without my feet. But I can carry you and drag you to the surface if I need to."

Something flashed in her eyes. Disappointment? Frustration? But whatever it was, within a second a flash of determination had wiped it from her face. Then as he watched, she leaned backward, braced her still-bound wrists against the sideways edge of what remained of her counter and pushed herself to her feet.

"We're not going to have a lot of time to grab things," she said. "Your bag is over by the bunk. There's a waterproof emergency kit under the counter with bottled water, a first-aid kit and a few other essentials. I don't see the laptop anywhere. I just wish we had time to save my computer and video files."

The fact she wasn't arguing with him bothered him. He didn't hear trust in her voice. If anything, he heard resignation. She seemed to be trying to loop the tape binding her wrists around the corner of the counter. He cut faster. The tape around his ankles was so thick, it was taking a lot longer than his hands had. Something inside his chest was practically screaming at him to free her hands and let her swim to safety. But the water was rising. There might only be time to free one of them. He couldn't swim without his legs, but if he needed to, he could save her. It was that simple. Trusting that she'd somehow save him would only get them both killed. The water was up to his neck now. The camper hit a rock. Rebecca was tossed back down into the water. A scream of frustration filled the camper.

"Just give me a second," he said. "One second. And then I'll save you."

But she was floundering in the water beside him and struggling to get back to her feet. Pale light streamed in from above them. Dark water swirled around her.

Maybe she wouldn't be able to save him.

But maybe he was willing to risk his life on saving her first.

Lord, I don't know if I'm doing the right thing here...

"Come here." He reached for her, wrapped his arm around her waist and pulled her onto his lap. With one arm he held her tight. Her chest pressed up against his chest. Her face was barely a breath away from his. He reached his other hand around her, until she was in between his arms. One hand held her bound hands out behind her back. The other hand slid the knife between her wrists. She leaned into him. Her head fell into the curve of his neck. He yanked the knife in one swift, hard cut, pulling it away from her body. The tape ripped. Her hands came free.

"Thank you." Her lips brushed his face and for the briefest of seconds his lips felt hers.

Then she grabbed ahold of the counter and scrambled to her feet.

"Go." He went back to hacking at his feet. "Grab what you need and climb onto the top of the camper. If you can make a clean jump, leap off and swim to shore. Look for rocks. Wood. Anything you can grab on to. Don't wait for me."

No answer. He looked back. She was yanking things from under the cabinet and stuffing them into his shoulder bag.

"Hurry up." The water was now up around his neck. He looked around for something to climb up on. If he didn't stand up he'd drown. If he stood up he wouldn't be able to free his feet. "I don't want you in here when the camper goes under."

Rebecca climbed around in front of him.

Water rose around her chest. The blade of a utility knife flashed in her hand.

"Like I'm going anywhere without you." She took a breath and dived underwater. Then he felt her hands on his. Her blade slid beside his, and the two knives worked together side by side to cut his legs free. The water rose over his head. The tape broke. *Thank You, God.* He shoved the kitchen knife into the bag and grabbed her hand.

They rose from the water together.

"Now, come on," he said. "I'll help you up onto the roof first. Then climb up after you."

"No, wait," she said. "I still need to find something."

Even standing the water was up to his chest and almost over her shoulders.

"You don't have time."

But she'd already shoved the bag into his hands. She dived back underwater. He slung the bag over his shoulder and looked up through the gap of the door above. They didn't have time to argue about this. The current was moving too quickly. They had to jump before the camper sank and they went under. Or the camper could roll and they'd drown. He leaped up, grabbed the open doorway with both hands and pulled himself through. The door broke off and spun away into the water. He crouched on the top of the camper. The river was wide. Trees lined the shore on both sides. Rocks filled the water, creating eddies and currents. They'd never make it to shore.

"We're going to need a raft," he shouted

down through the hole where the door had been. "Anything to help us float."

"Here!" She yanked the camper's wooden tabletop out and shoved it through the hole. "It's not much, but it'll float. Should hold us both up for a little while."

He took it from her hands, braced it under his knees and reached down through the doorway. "Now, come on. Grab my arms and I'll pull you up."

No answer. He looked down. Rebecca was still rummaging around in the water.

"Come on! Look, I get it. It's your whole life in there. I know it's going to hurt to lose it. But we don't have time to be sentimental!"

The water was now inches from the doorway. But it was like she didn't even hear him. Rebecca dived underwater again. He glanced ahead. They were nearing a bend in the river. Large rocks loomed ahead. Reluctantly, he shifted the tabletop into his left hand, leaving just his right hand for her to grab.

"Whatever you're looking for, leave it. We'll find a way to survive without it!"

"Got it!" She grabbed his outstretched arm.

The water swirled over her head. He yanked her up through the hole. The camper disappeared into the water beneath them. Surging water threatened to pull her from his grasp.

Her hand tightened in his. He shoved the tabletop under their arms and they held it like an oversized flutter board.

They spun in the current. A flat rock loomed ahead of them by the shoreline. He steered them toward it. Their legs kicked hard against the pull of the river. Then he felt rock smack hard against his knees and he braced his legs against it. Water beat against his body, threatening to carry them downriver. Rebecca scrambled up the rock, using his arms and shoulders like a ladder. He crawled up after her. They lay there a moment on the slippery outcrop of the water's edge.

Prayer poured from their lips, mingling together with the sound of rushing water.

Then he pulled himself to his feet.

"Whatever you went back for, I hope it was worth risking your life for."

Then he looked down. The words froze on his lips as an odd bitterness filled his mouth.

She was clutching her high school martial arts trophy.

She lay there a moment on the slippery rock face, staring at the deep blue waters that had just swallowed her camper.

Lord, I know I should probably pray right now, but I don't know what to pray.

Tears filled her eyes. It was the only real home she'd had. The only place she'd ever fallen asleep at night feeling totally at home and totally at peace. Growing up, it had been as if her mother had always been on a knife's edge waiting for word from the father Rebecca had never even met. Then they'd become "the Miles family" and the house had felt even less like a place where she actually belonged.

"Seth said he came to me for help." She said the words out loud but didn't know exactly if she was talking to Zack or herself. Her hand still clenched the cheap, gold-coated trophy so tightly she could feel it digging into her skin, and she didn't even know why she'd grabbed it.

"He told me he'd been trying to do the right thing," she said, "trying to help people and right a wrong. But it had all blown up in his face and someone had been shot. So he'd come running to me. Because he thought I was the only one who would listen or understand."

Why, Lord? She prayed. *Why did he think I'd listen? Because he thought I was weak and foolish? Because he thought he could use me?*

She looked back at the water, as if staring at it hard enough would suddenly make her camper rise from the depths like a phoenix.

"Come on," Zack said softly. His hand touched her shoulder. "Let's get off this rock."

There was about a four-foot gap between the edge of the rock and the riverbank, but enough smaller rocks filling the gap to make stepping stones. Zack jumped over first and then stretched his arm out to help her. But his eyes were on her feet, not her face. When she grabbed his hand, his fingers didn't loop through hers, and when she reached the shore, he let go immediately and stepped back a couple of feet.

"Okay," he said. "So, let's see what's in the bag and take stock of what we have. Then we'll make a plan and plot our course from there. I suggest you take your shoes and socks off. The sooner you get dry, the healthier you'll be."

He pulled off his own sweatshirt, shoes and socks and carefully laid them on a rock by the water's edge, where the rising sun touched the ground. She dropped the trophy on the ground. She didn't even know why she'd grabbed it. Her whole world had been sinking around her and suddenly she'd remembered Seth yelling to remember her trophy.

"Seth did a lot of talking after you lay down in the bunk," she said. "I don't remember all of it. Probably because he'd drugged the soup. The stuff I do remember doesn't make a lot of sense."

"I wouldn't bother trying to make sense of it.

Seth's a criminal and a liar. He's always been rotten to the core." Zack sat down and started methodically emptying the bag and her emergency kit onto a dry and sheltered patch of ground. He had always known more about surviving in the Canadian wilderness than anyone she'd ever met. Her brain knew there was absolutely no better person for her to be in this with. But still, something felt off between them. Something she couldn't put a finger on.

"We have a small, palm-size video camera," he said. "Not that I can see us needing it, but I get why you'd have one in your emergency kit. I hope for your sake it's waterproof."

"It is." She pulled off her shoes and socks and set them beside Zack's.

Years ago, while everyone else in class had just left their shoes in a heap in the hallway outside martial arts, she and Zack had always brought their shoes in with them and set them side by side at the edge of the mats, after Seth had once filled them with pancake syrup. Zack had the same shoe size now that he'd had then, and his soles were still scuffed and worn the same way, too. Her gaze ran over the solid strength of the man now sitting on the ground under the base of a tree. The strength of his arms shone in the rising sun. Then her gaze lingered on his bare feet, wedged underneath him, crossed in the same way he'd always crossed them back when they used to sit together.

"Some fire-starting papers," he went on, "four granola bars, a canteen we can fill with water..."

He'd gone from being the kind of boy the other girls had overlooked to being the kind of man who probably turned heads when he walked into a room. New and improved Zack was exactly the person she needed in a crisis. There wasn't a doubt in her mind about that. But, somehow, right now, old Zack was the person she longed for. The guy who would've had his arms around her right now, hugging her tightly.

She reached down and picked up the martial arts trophy. Sun caught the gold-plated metal, sending a flash of light across Zack's eyes. He frowned, then started patting down his pockets. Funny how light the trophy was. That was the first thing she'd noticed when she'd stumbled up to the podium to collect it. After years of seeing trophies and medals collecting dust on Seth's shelf, she'd expected it to feel more substantial than that.

"As for usable things we have on our persons," he said, "we've got a utility knife, a kitchen knife, two leather belts, four pairs of shoelaces… Do you have anything else I haven't thought of?"

A high school trophy. That Seth had insisted she remember.

She turned the trophy around. "Can you pass me the knife? I have a thought."

He raised an eyebrow and handed it over. She stuck it between the base and the small metal cup on top and pried it off. There was nothing there, just a solid piece of wood. Okay then, so Seth hadn't hidden anything in the base. But the cup felt hollow. She shook it. Nothing. She laid it down on the ground, picked up a rock and smashed the cup in half.

There was nothing there.

She sat back and sighed, and tossed it in the dirt.

"You want to tell me what that was all about?" Zack said.

"The last thing I remember Seth shouting before I blacked out was that I had to remember this trophy, no matter what happened next, that I shouldn't forget it. He'd been so insistent about it, I wondered if he'd hidden something inside it. But it's empty."

Zack snorted. "I can't believe you let Seth play you like that. He was probably just trying to upset you and drive a wedge between us by dredging up ancient history."

Okay, he had a point, and usually she'd be the very last person to defend her stepbrother.

"But he sounded panicked," she said. "He'd been yelling it. Like it mattered a lot. You should've heard it."

"But I didn't hear it, because he *drugged* me and then tried to manipulate you and take advantage of your good nature."

"Yes, but he wasn't like normal Seth. He was different, panicked. First he said my stepfather sent Black Talon after me. Then he took it back and said he hadn't meant to say that at all. But that he had written the blog about how the General was a philanderer and the person who'd convinced him to steal the computer program contacted him through the blog. I'm guessing because they figured he had no respect for the military or respecting people's privacy. Sometime in all that I think he also sang a medley of show tunes."

Zack just stared. Okay, so it did sound kind of crazy when she tried to explain it like that.

"But then, when I started passing out, and Black Talon, or whoever it was, started coming through the woods to kidnap us, he hissed in my ear something like, 'Remember the trophy you got the night you thought Zack stood you up.'"

"What do you mean?" Zack said. "I never stood you up."

As if that mattered now.

"Yes, you did," she said. "Remember? You invited me to go to the sports banquet with you. I'd thought it was a date. I went to a hairdresser and bought some stupidly expensive dress. Spent all the money I had saved. Then I waited around for, like, an hour by the front door for you. You didn't show. I cried buckets. But hey, I was seventeen and nobody had ever asked me out before."

Zack stood up slowly. His lips set in a grim line. His face looked so pained, she thought for a moment he was going to be sick.

"Sorry, I'm not trying to upset you. Just being honest. Eventually, Seth took pity on me and insisted I go to the banquet with him. They were just serving the main course when I got there. It was probably, like, the one decent thing he'd ever done."

Zack ran his hand over his face.

"Of course." His head shook. "Of course you did…of course he did…I should've… Of course… *Forgive me*...I was such an idiot…"

"I don't understand." Why was Zack so upset? That night was ancient history and he'd known what had happened better than anyone.

"So, you decided to stay home and apply for

the military instead of going. We were both really young. I know you never meant to hurt me."

Zack slid his arms down to his sides and looked at her straight on. "Seth came over to my house earlier that night and told me you were canceling our date."

Her heart dropped through her stomach. The pain felt just as acute as if that one night twenty years ago had somehow crashed straight through the barrier of time and landed in the moment in which they stood. "Oh no..."

"Oh yes." There was a bitter edge to Zack's voice. A decades-old ache filled his eyes. "Seth told me that you had only agreed to go to the banquet with me because you felt sorry for me. Because I was so emotional and sensitive, you were afraid to say anything because you didn't want to hurt me. So he said he'd decided to step up and tell me to stay away from you. Because a fat slob like me wasn't good enough for a girl like you, and I'd never amount to anything in life, and you knew it."

I was trying to protect you from Zack, Seth had said. *He wasn't good enough for you. So I stepped up and showed you what kind of guy he really was.*

Her head was shaking. For a moment she wanted to cry. She wanted to hug him. She wanted to find Seth and strangle him. No wonder Zack hadn't picked her up. No wonder he'd signed up for the military that night.

"You believed him," she said.

"Of course I believed him!" Zack's voice rose. "He was right, wasn't he? I was out of shape, eating my feelings, going nowhere. I hardly had a mature handle on anything in my life. I'd wanted to be in the military. I'd wanted to be special forces. I'd wanted to be the man I am now. Seth's words might've been cruel, but they gave me the kick I needed to make it happen. So after he left, I changed out of my suit, sat down and signed up for the army."

And then he'd run through the pouring rain to angrily, defiantly tell her that he'd done it. Not because he'd rejected her. But because he thought she'd rejected him.

She stepped toward him. "You should've told me."

Zack crossed his arms across his chest. "Well, he was right, wasn't he? You were so beautiful, Becs! You were tenacious and kind and smart and strong. Any man would've been blessed to have you. I was hardly the guy you deserved."

"Yes, you were." Her hand brushed along his crossed arms; she wished they'd open, that they'd hold her. "You were the guy that I'd wanted."

You're the only guy I've ever wanted. Even before I knew how incredible you are now and how you'd changed your life. Why can't you see that?

He looked at her for a very long moment, as if he was weighing what his next words should be.

"Thank you," he said finally. "It means a lot that you thought so highly of me."

Zack bent down and started scooping their belongings back into the bag, including her broken trophy. "I'm not sorry I joined the military and made the changes to my life I did. But I regret getting so wound up that night and not handling my conversation with you better. And I apologize for not calling to confirm I wasn't coming and leaving you without a ride to the sports banquet. That was rude of me."

That was it? That was all he was going to say?

"Now, come on," he said. "I suggest we follow the river. Judging by the sun in the sky it's flowing southeast and if we keep going that way we'll eventually hit civilization. We should both make sure we're well hydrated." He filled the water bottle from the river and offered it to her. "I think we should split a granola bar for breakfast, if that's okay with you. I can run on pretty low fuel, but I don't think either of us should be on an empty stomach."

She took a long drink of water and handed the bottle back. He finished it.

"Now, I need to think." He slid the bottle back into the bag. "I don't know who we can trust right now and I've got to be smart in how I plan our next move."

He started walking. She followed. So that was it? They were going to confess all that to each other, and then he was just going to shut it down and change the subject?

Realizing that Zack hadn't meant to break her heart and that Seth had sabotaged their date that night meant everything to her. But apparently, it meant nothing to Zack.

They kept walking. Zack was silent. The river grew wider.

She started to hum, then sing show tunes under her breath. The weird little medley Seth had been singing outside the camper when she'd been drugged still spun in her mind like an earworm she couldn't shake. "Maria. Maria in the winter..."

Zack stopped walking dead in his tracks, so suddenly she nearly walked into his back. "What did you just sing?"

There was a look on his face she couldn't quite read.

"Just some silly thing that Seth kept singing, round and round. I'm sorry, I guess it got stuck in my head."

"And you're sure those are the exact words he was singing?"

"I think so." She shrugged.

"Think, Rebecca. It's important." Zack's hands touched her shoulders lightly. He turned her toward him. "What exactly did Seth sing? What was the context? Why did he sing it?"

There was an edge to his voice she'd never heard before. A hard edge. A dangerous edge. As if she alone knew the secret password to unlocking a major weapon and he was waiting on her to confirm it.

She closed her eyes. "He was singing songs with the name Maria in them. Then he asked if I'd ever heard of Maria, and that was the name of the woman who'd contacted him and told him to steal something from the government computer to prove my stepfather was a bad person." She opened her eyes. "But I don't see how that matters, considering the woman who came to meet him in the park was really just a Black Talon operative and not actually this Maria person."

Zack's hands tightened on her shoulders. "Did he tell you where Maria was now?"

She shook her head. "No. He thought she was dead, remember? Why?"

"I can't tell you why. Not until I'm certain. Did he tell you her last name?"

"No. He didn't tell me anything more than that. He just said her name was Maria, and then sang something like, 'Maria in the winter, Maria in the snow, snow, snow.'"

"Snow?" Zack's face paled. He closed his eyes. "Oh, God," he prayed. "Oh, God, have mercy."

"What?" She grabbed his hands as they fell from her shoulders. "Zack? What? You're scaring me. Does this all mean something to you?"

"It means I think I might actually know what it was that your stepbrother stole and got downloaded on your laptop, and why Black Talon members would kill each other to get their hands on it." He opened his eyes. "And it's a cyberweapon."

ELEVEN

Shock spread like cold water over Rebecca's limbs. "You're telling me that my stepbrother stole a cyberweapon from the Canadian government, and two factions of a European gang are willing to kidnap and murder to get it?"

"I'm saying that it's possible," Zack said. "Certainly I can't rule out the possibility."

She'd never seen fear in his eyes before. Not like this. But she could see a faint glimmer of it there now, and that terrified her. "That sounds like something you shouldn't tell me."

He didn't answer. He looked at her for a long moment.

"Maybe," he said, finally. "But I trust you, and my top priority right now is telling you what you need to know for everyone to get out of this alive."

Then they started walking again. His footsteps were quicker now. His long legs strode through the trees. Questions flew through her mind so quickly, it was as if she could feel them crashing into each other. What kind of cyberweapon? What was it? What did it do?

But somehow as she looked at Zack, she felt something inside her shift. He was concerned, worried, as if he was carrying knowledge he didn't want to carry. And somehow, seeing that look in his eyes told her everything she needed to know.

Her hand brushed his arm. "It's okay, if you can't tell me more than that. I understand you can't tell me everything I want to know."

"Thanks. I really appreciate that." He swallowed hard. Then he took her hand in his and squeezed it tightly for a long moment before letting it fall. "So much more than you know."

They kept walking in silence, side by side over the rocky shore by the river's edge.

Zack pulled an old-looking silver medallion from his wallet, spun it slowly between his fingers and then slid it open sideways. He held it up in front of him, as if trying to get their bearings. It was a compass of some sort, with a small pedometer underneath. He turned left and started walking through the trees.

Her legs ached. Sweat ran down her neck. She used the utility knife to cut a thin slit of fabric off the bottom of her sweatshirt and twisted it into a headband to tie her hair back.

But even still bugs swarmed her skin. Zack's fingers brushed the back of her neck, then pinched her skin softly. The gesture was sweet, strong, comforting.

"Mosquito," he said. "I killed it before it could get you."

"Thank you."

He paused. Then said, "I need you to trust me. What qualifies as 'need to know' has shifted a lot in the last couple of hours, and I don't think it helps either of us for me to keep you in the dark. I'm pretty much convinced of that. But—"

"But you still can't tell me what you can't tell me."

"Right." He smiled. "Thanks. And you can't repeat what I tell you. Not to anyone. Ever. Okay?"

She nodded. "Understood."

"A while back, I went into a hostile Eastern European country to extract a young computer engineer, who'd contacted our government seeking asylum," he said. "Literally nabbed her off a crowded street, in broad daylight, when she'd gone on a coffee run for her office. I had her out of the country and over the border in hours. She was in her early twenties and had grown up in a particularly unpleasant orphanage. But still, she left everything behind to come to Canada. Everything."

Rebecca nodded slowly. Again, why was he telling her this? She could tell it was important. She didn't know why.

"This young woman was truly brilliant. She'd developed a decryption program that was intended to revolutionize cybersafety. You know how you have passwords for everything online?"

She nodded. "Yes, and Seth keeps hacking them."

"Well, imagine living in a country where the government asks people like Seth to create a computer program that gives them the power to systematically hack into people's accounts," he said. "To overwrite your password with one of their own, so that you can't get into your account anymore, but they can. Giving them complete access to any account they want. But not just email accounts. Banking. Financial institutions. Other militaries' secrets and weapon launch codes."

Her heart stopped. "Oh."

"Imagine your own government found you in an orphanage, realized how talented you were, sent you to school and trained you. But then in return expected you to create a computer program like that for them. But then a dangerous organized criminal group discovered you had it, too, and wanted it for themselves."

Black Talon.

"Suddenly two different factions inside this one gang are both terrorizing you," he added. "Maybe you suspect the criminals have people planted in your work or your apartment building. But then, so might your own government. Maybe a mercenary kidnaps you for a couple of days and threatens to hurt you unless you give them the program once you're done. But your own government isn't much better and you figure that no matter who gets ahold of this program, you're dead. So, you contact the local Canadian embassy and beg them for asylum in return for giving them the program and keeping it out of enemy hands. Then some guy like me extracts you and gets you to Canada."

The sound of the river disappeared in the distance.

Zack turned to face her. "Now, imagine this whole thing is so classified that even a guy like me isn't allowed to know anything about this. Because this whole situation is above *my* pay grade. I only know it because I spent three hours driving through hostile territory with you, wedged in a secret compartment inside my dashboard, and you kept blurting out things that I wasn't allowed to know. So I never told anyone. Not my colleagues. Not Jeff, my commanding officer. I just get you safely on a plane and erase everything you told me from my mind."

She closed her eyes and let the pieces of what Zack was telling her fall into place.

"She told me to call her Maria Snow," he said. "I think Maria might've been her real first name. But the *Snow* part was clearly fake. She was beautiful and brilliant, and reminded me of you in a lot of ways. I can't imagine she'd come to Canada only to throw her lot in with Black Talon criminals and I have no idea why she'd ever contact Seth and tell him about the decryption program. But there's only two ways Seth could've heard the name *Maria Snow.* Either someone in the Canadian military leaked that information to whoever in Black Talon impersonated her, or Seth was actually contacted by the real Maria Snow, who for some reason decided to blow the deal she made with the people who rescued her."

He looked down at the compass and suddenly she realized it wasn't pointing north. It was pointing somewhere else entirely, and the pedometer at the bottom seemed to be counting down. Wherever he was taking them, it was now less than fourteen thousand steps away.

"I'm telling you this so you get what's at stake," he added. "I'm telling you this so you understand why I'm about to take the action I'm about to take and so that you're clear what our situation is. I need you to trust me." He flipped the compass upside down and flicked the bottom open. Inside was a tiny key. "And to do that, I need to trust you."

After another hour, they'd hit a rural highway and started to pass by the occasional business or farmhouse. Occasionally a vehicle would slow and ask if they needed a ride. But Zack just slung his arm casually around Rebecca's shoulders, kept his head down and avoided eye contact. Rebecca did the same.

Eventually he spotted a dilapidated gas station and convenience store at the side of the highway. Paint was peeling on the white shutters. Torn and faded posters were slapped along the side. There were only two cars filling up and nobody else in sight but a scruffy-looking teenager with a backpack bigger than he was, smoking on a bench next to a crude hitchhiking sign.

"I need to try to make a phone call," Zack said. "I'm taking you to the Shields' island house. Think of it like an unofficial safe house. I don't want to show up unannounced, if I can help it, even though to be honest I'm not sure they're even in the country. While I'm on the phone, how about you try to fill up the water bottle?"

She nodded, gave him a quick kiss on the cheek and then headed around the side of the building. He pulled his hoodie over his head and walked to the pay phone beside the convenience store. He lifted the receiver and was relieved to get a dial tone.

"Hey, hey. You heading south?" the teenager with the backpack shouted at Zack. He sauntered across the parking lot. "Give me a ride? Eh? A ride? A ride?"

Zack shook his head. "Sorry."

"How 'bout some money, then? Get me something to eat?"

The young man was now standing so close, Zack could smell what he'd been smoking. Zack reached into his bag, pulled out a granola bar and fixed him with a look that made it clear that was all he was going to get. The hitchhiker turned up his nose and walked off.

Zack turned back to the phone and dialed. It rang. He waited three rings, depressed the plunger and got his coins back. Then he tried again. Three more rings. Then he hung up.

Come on, Mark. Be there. Get the signal.

A very long time ago, when Mark was a

young man coming up in the world and Zack was his former bodyguard, Mark had started taking overseas charity trips into danger zones. They'd set up three sets of three rings as a private code that meant, *I'm in danger. I need help. Whatever I say when I answer could be under duress.*

As the head of an international-development charity, Mark had used the private code to call Zack just a handful of times over the past twenty years, usually to get his advice on exiting a tricky situation quickly and safely. No matter where Mark and his wife, Katie, had been in the world, Zack usually knew something—a church that was safe, a route that tended to be not that heavily monitored or a family they could trust.

Zack had never once used the signal to call Mark.

The phone rang three times, for the third and final time.

Okay, now to place the call for real. A car pulled into the parking lot. He waited, holding the phone in his hand while the couple entered the convenience store. The sound of a voice on television slipped through the open door.

"...obviously, it's disappointing. As a parent you do the best you can. I was just thankful to hear that horrid gossip-mongering blog about my family has finally been shut down. The last thing our country needs right now is a salacious distraction from the good work the men and women in uniform are doing..."

Zack glanced at the screen. General Arthur Miles was front and center on the twenty-four-hour news station, in full uniform. The door clattered shut, muffling the General's voice.

But still Zack could read the subtitles. The interviewer was asking him about the charges against Seth.

"You need to understand that I was never close to my stepdaughter, Rebecca," the General was saying. "Her mother, my second wife, was a prescription drug addict who died due to her addiction. There's every indication that her daughter, Rebecca, is now an addict herself, and that my son, Seth, is currently under Rebecca's influence. It's very upsetting. But he's always been weak."

Zack felt his jaw drop. General Miles was throwing Rebecca under the bus? Why? Because he honestly knew so little about his late wife's daughter? Or because it was easier to save face by telling lies than by admitting his son was his own man who'd chosen to become a thief and a criminal?

In all the times he'd heard General Miles's speech-making, whether on television or before a rapt military crowd, he'd never once heard the General say something that Zack had known for a fact was untrue. Not until now. Something about watching the General talk about Rebecca that way, with such candor and ease, shook Zack to the core. An honorable man should not be able to tell unfounded untruths so easily. Doing so effortlessly took practice.

General Miles turned to face the camera, his crisp white hair and clipped white mustache standing out on his suntanned face.

Zack felt his fists clench at his side.

"Rebecca, if you can hear me, turn yourself in. Return what you stole. Get the help you need."

The screen changed. The television screen flashed a bright red bulletin with rolling text: "Canadian homegrown terrorist plot. Suspects wanted. General Arthur Miles 'gutted' and offers reward for information."

Then three faces flashed side by side on the screen, along with the text: "Seth Miles. Rebecca Miles. Sergeant Zachary Keats. Wanted for murder, treason and suspected terrorist activities."

The phone fell from Zack's hands. He stepped back, gasping for breath, as if he'd just been shot in the chest.

Zack was a wanted man. A fugitive.

He'd been branded a traitor.

"Hey, hey. Pretty girl. Why aren't you smiling? Give me a smile." The hitchhiker was harassing someone else now. Then Zack saw Rebecca, walking down the side of the building by the garbage cans. Her head was down. Her arms were crossed. The scruffy young man walked so close behind her that he was almost stepping on her feet. "Come on, girl. Just give me some money. You've got money right? Just give me twenty. Twenty. You got twenty? Ten? You got ten?"

Rebecca spun toward him. "Back off and leave me alone."

"Hey. You heard her." Zack strode toward them, feeling the hood fall from his head. "Leave her alone."

"This is none of your business." The young man scowled. "This is between her and me. And we're cool. Right, girl? You and me. We're just talking."

Then his eyes narrowed.

"Hey, I know you. I know both of you." He looked from Rebecca to Zack. "You're those thieves on the news who stole some stuff, right? Money? Drugs? Something? You give me a cut of whatever it was right now or I'm calling for the cops and getting that reward."

Zack nearly rolled his eyes. Some delusional drug-addled hitchhiker was the last thing they needed right now.

Zack nodded to Rebecca. “You good to go?”

“Yeah,” she said, “I got the bottle filled. Let’s get out of here.”

She started toward him.

“Hey, not so fast.” A knife flashed in the hitchhiker’s hand. He grabbed Rebecca by the hair. The knife hovered toward her throat. “Give me a cut of whatever it was you guys stole or she’s getting it in the neck.”

Zack tensed his muscles to charge. But before he’d even taken a step, he watched as Rebecca deflected the blade, spun on her heel and knocked the hitchhiker to the ground in one quick, seamless move. Then she kicked the knife out of the dazed man’s hands, sending it flying in behind the garbage cans. Zack nearly whistled.

And that’s why her trophy read “Technically Flawless.”

She glanced at Zack. “We’re running now, right?”

“Yup.” Zack grabbed Rebecca’s hand. They ran for the tree line.

“Hey! Stop them! Somebody! Call 911! They’re criminals, right?” they could hear the hitchhiker screaming behind them.

Zack's hand tightened in hers. They sprinted through the underbrush. His ears strained, listening for footsteps. Nobody followed. Finally their footsteps slowed. He looked back. Silence.

"Thank You, God," he prayed. Then he slid his arms around Rebecca's waist and hugged her tightly. "That was amazing. You are amazing."

He half expected her to pull away. But instead she stayed there. His hands on her back. Her arms around his body. Their hearts pounding together. His lips brushed the top of her head.

"I hate seeing you in danger, even though I know you can handle yourself." He pulled her closer. "I really, really hate it."

"I don't exactly like it when you're in danger, either." She raised her face toward his.

His mouth hovered just a breath away from hers and it took all the self-control in his body to not kiss her. His heart muscles ached with the knowledge that she was the bravest, strongest, most beautiful person he'd ever seen in his life. He'd never met anyone better. He suspected that he never would. He knew he didn't want to.

"Why did he call us thieves?" she asked.

"Because that's what the media's calling us.

You, me and Seth. They're saying all three of us are traitors, killers and thieves." He let go and stepped back. "That means I have to report back to base and turn myself in."

She reached for his hands and looped her fingers through his. "I'm going with you."

"No, you're not." He pulled his hands away and slid them in his pockets. "It's not safe. It's almost nine hours to Ottawa from here. Anything could happen on the road."

"I'll be safer with you than I will be without you."

"No, it'll be safer for both of us if I get you to the safe house and I travel alone. You rattle my brain, Rebecca. You rattle my thinking when I need to focus on the situation at hand. We'll both be safer if I travel solo. I'll get you to Mark and Katie's house, borrow a vehicle from them and make my way to base. Then I'll tell someone I trust your location, that you're surrendering and where to find you. Trust me. It's safer this way. For both of us."

He leaned forward to brush his lips over the top of her head.

He meant the gesture to be comforting. But before he could kiss her, she stepped back.

"Well, then," she said, "I'd guess we'd better get going."

He pulled his compass out of his pocket. They were less than half an hour away now.

"There's something else you should know," he said as they walked, "which I'm really sorry to tell you, because I can't imagine how horrible this must be to hear. General Miles, your stepfather, was just on the television in the convenience store. He said the blog Seth created about him has been shut down. Not that he acknowledged Seth as its creator. He also accused you of manipulating Seth and of being, and I'm quoting here, a drug addict like your mother."

The lack of shock on her face told him more about her life as a member of the General's family than he'd ever wanted to know.

"My mother got hooked on prescription drugs because she couldn't handle not being able to trust him." Rebecca's gaze focused on the trees ahead. "I know in your eyes, in everyone's eyes, he's a well-respected man and a military hero. But to me, he was just the cold stranger who took over my life. I honestly don't know why my mother married him or what was going on in their marriage, let alone his marriage to Seth's mother. Just that she felt when she married him that she had to be the perfect military housewife and sit around the house, knitting blankets and sewing curtains, waiting for him to come home. She was so miserable. She couldn't handle it. The anxiety. The stress. The secrets. Having no life at all besides waiting for her husband to come home." Her voice dropped. "I always promised myself I wouldn't be one of those women. I told myself that wouldn't be me."

Just because that was her life as a military spouse doesn't mean it has to be yours. Life as a military spouse could be whatever you want it to be. I've met military spouses who are firefighters and chefs and artists and teachers and very happy parents and homemakers. Both my parents served. As did both my uncle and aunt, in different branches.

But while he could hear the words in his head, he didn't speak them. What good would it do? To try to talk Rebecca into a life she didn't want.

A life he wasn't sure he was ready for her to want.

They kept going, keeping off the roads and pausing at every whisper of wind in the trees. Eventually they reached a long, narrow lake. They stood and looked out to where a small island rose from the water. A house stood in the middle, made of beautiful arching wood and sweeping glass windows. A small powerboat was docked out front.

"You think you can swim that?" Zack asked. "It's about a twenty-minute swim. If not, I'll go get the powerboat and come back for you."

Rebecca eyed the distance for a long moment. Then she slipped off her shoes and rolled her blue jeans up all the way to her knees, showing off strong, shapely legs. Her muscles were definitely more toned than when he'd known her last.

"Yeah, I can," she said. "No problem."

They swam, side by side. Their bodies cut through the crisp water in the late-morning sunshine. He watched her as they swam. Just little sideways glances. He'd never seen anyone more beautiful, and with every stroke, he regretted pulling away from her the way that he had. He hated to have to leave her again. Some of the other people he knew in the unit had husbands or wives. A few had children. One or two even had grandchildren.

Would it be possible to have a relationship with a woman like her without it ruining his focus when he was out on a mission? Maybe his heart muscle was strong enough to handle it now. But then, even if it were possible, how could he ever do that to her? Rebecca had just lost everything she owned. How could he ever ask her to spend her life waiting for him while he traveled around the world, never knowing where he was or when he was getting back? How could he ask her to choose the same life that had so hurt her mother?

Finally, he felt the water get shallow underneath him. His feet touched the sand. He stretched out his hand, reached for Rebecca's and pulled her to him. They stumbled to shore. "Come on, let's get in the door and dried off."

The metallic sound of hunting rifle's bolt slamming shut made the words freeze in his mouth.

"Stop right there," a woman's voice said. "Or trust me, I'll shoot."

TWELVE

Rebecca's hand grabbed hold of Zack's, instinctively feeling for his strength and awaiting his lead. A stunning woman with long taffy-blond hair stepped out from behind a tree in jeans, a tank top and an open plaid shirt. Her stomach swelled in the tight, compact ball of a third-trimester pregnancy. Her steady hands leveled the rifle at their heads.

"Hey, Katie." Zack's arm slipped around Rebecca's waist. They were still standing knee-deep in water. "This is my friend Rebecca Miles. Rebecca, this is Katie Shields, codirector of Shield Trust International Development."

Rebecca knew exactly who she was. The Shields were famous in the global charity world for inventing and building low-cost technical solutions to help local groups in developing countries help their own communities. They were considered on the cutting edge of sustainable overseas development work. Mark was a former angry and rebellious rich boy turned philanthropist. Katie was a journalist who'd survived a terrifying murder plot. It wasn't an exaggeration to call them heroes of hers.

Which didn't begin to explain why Katie was still holding a gun on Zack.

Zack didn't even acknowledge the gun. Instead he just smiled and stood there calmly with his arm around the bedraggled mess that was Rebecca, as if this was the welcome he'd expected.

"Hey, Zack." Katie smiled faintly. "Mind telling me the name of Mark's current portable radio device?"

A wry smile curled at just one corner of his lips. "Officially, it's known as Noah's Arc. But since the very first prototype went up in an impressive ball of flames a few years back—just between you and me—your husband tends to refer to it as Old Smokey. The model he's currently working on is, I believe, Smokey Three?"

"Smokey Four, actually." A smile spread from her lips up into the lights of her eyes. She lowered the rifle and stretched out her hand toward Rebecca. "Welcome to my island, Rebecca. It's so nice to meet you."

Rebecca stepped to shore and took her outstretched hand. Even with ragged jeans and without a spot of makeup on her skin, Katie seemed to shine with a light that made Rebecca feel self-conscious, like an awkward sister.

"I've been watching the television news coverage about your situation," Katie added. "I'm glad Zack knew you could come here for help."

"Thank you," Rebecca said. "It's an honor to meet you. I've been following your work."

She expected a handshake, but instead Katie gave her a soft, friendly hug.

Then Katie turned to Zack. "Zack, old man! About time you came to visit!"

"Hey, you." Zack smiled. "Why the firing-squad welcome? Since when do you put friends through security questions?"

"Are you kidding me?" She laughed. "Like I said, I've been following the news. Your name is being splashed all over the media as a wanted man. Then you put through an emergency-signal phone call to Mark earlier and never called back. I had to make sure you weren't under duress and being held against your will."

Rebecca's jaw dropped. "You were testing Zack to make sure *I* wasn't holding him against his will?"

Had Katie not noticed the strength in Zack's arms? Or the total size differential between them?

Katie laughed. "Let's just say I learned a long time ago not to underestimate anyone."

Rebecca glanced at Zack, but his eyes just twinkled. He stepped up onto the shore and ran one hand through his sopping hair. "Oh, Becs could totally best me under the right circumstances."

A flush rose to her cheeks. Was he teasing? Or serious?

Katie handed Rebecca the rifle, and then hugged Zack tightly. He laid one hand protectively over Katie's back, like an older brother. Then he let her go.

"Why didn't you tell me you two were now building a baby Shields?" he asked.

"Because Mark wanted to tell you in person," she said, "and you two haven't managed to be in the same country together in almost a year."

"So, where is your husband?" Zack asked.

"Not here." Katie led the way up the stone path to the house. "He's out in the field this week. Middle East specifically. Meeting with a group of refugees about a development project. I don't expect him back for a couple more days."

"And you're here holding down the fort," Zack said.

"Pretty much." Katie wiped her boots off on the welcome mat. "I'd have gone with him, but I'm due in six weeks and my doctor would not let me get on the airplane. Now, just leave your wet shoes by the door and I'll go find something clean and dry for you to change into."

Katie disappeared into the house. Rebecca rolled her eyes. Here was a prime example of the kind of life she wanted to avoid. This woman was heavily pregnant, and left alone while her husband ran around overseas in unsafe countries. Zack shook his head and chuckled a little. He tilted his head toward Rebecca.

"I can tell what you're thinking," he whispered, "and you're wrong."

Rebecca turned toward Zack, "You don't know what I'm thinking."

"Yeah." He smiled. "I kind of think I do. You're thinking about our conversation about women like your mother who sit around at home, miserably sewing blankets and curtains, or however you put it, with no life of their own, just waiting for their husbands to come home. You're presuming that Katie is one of them."

She shrugged, and didn't deny it. He chuckled.

"What?" she asked.

"It's just, if you knew Katie you'd know how funny it is that anyone would think that about her. Katie is the strongest, most intelligent, most fiercely independent woman I've ever met. Well, one of the two of them, that is."

He shot her a sideways glance that sent heat through her chest.

"Mark is my best friend on the planet," he went on. "Strong heart, brilliant mind. You will never meet a better man. But he's also a stubborn, absentminded inventor, who's great at anything that has to do with electronics and moving parts, but whose company would've totally failed financially if he hadn't had the smarts to fall in love with Katie and let her take the reins of the management and communications side. And he'd be the first person to tell you that."

He pushed the door open. "Besides, if you think 'holding down the fort' is somehow a lesser job than being 'out in the field,' then it's only because you have no idea just how impressive this fort really is."

He was still chuckling as they walked through the door. She stepped through the front door, expecting to see a typical living room. Instead, she found herself in a huge, beautiful open space that was a family room, library, office and study in one. Towering wood beams crossed above her head. Warm brown couches and reclaimed wood furniture nestled in a sunken living room to her left. Straight ahead lay a dining table, large enough to seat twelve, with an open pass-through space to the kitchen behind it, and a hallway that she guessed led to the bedrooms. To her right were two huge desks, overflowing with several computers of different shapes and sizes, and at least five different screens, all of which seemed to be humming. Every inch of space seemed to be covered in papers, books or electronic components. But there was something about the clutter that somehow didn't make it feel messy. Rather the space felt very loved, very homey and very safe in a way she couldn't put her finger on.

But something about the way Zack was still grinning at her almost made her defensive. What was his point exactly? That it was possible to be happy and married to a strong man without ending up like her mother? But so what? There was only one strong man she'd ever imagined herself married to. And he didn't want her for a wife.

Tension rose to the back of her neck. "Katie may be doing an amazing job of running her husband's business. But she still gave up her dream, of being a journalist, to run his company."

"Actually," Katie's voice came from the doorway in the back of the room, "I gave up my job of being a journalist and my hope of becoming an editor for the job of corunning and co-owning a company." She walked into the room with an armful of clothes. A smile curved on her lips. "And yup, I'm in love with and married to the other co-owner, which has its own pluses and minuses." She laughed. "More pluses than minuses."

An uncomfortable heat rose to Rebecca's cheeks. Katie's eyes met Rebecca's. There was a softness there, an understanding, a forgiveness even that Rebecca wasn't expecting.

Katie walked over to the desk, opened a drawer and pulled out a huge, heavy-looking phone. She handed it to Zack. "Use this. Call whoever you need to call. It's a prototype Mark was working on, so it's both untraceable and disposable. We've been calling back and forth on it while he tries to work out some kinks in the system, so if it starts ringing, it's probably him. You left a pair of fatigues in our washing machine last time you were here. They're in the top drawer in the guest room."

Zack nodded, took the phone and headed down the hall, leaving Katie and Rebecca alone in the room.

"These clothes are mine." Katie held up a pair of jeans, a navy sweatshirt and a T-shirt for Rebecca. "But they should fit you."

"I'm so sorry for what I said." Rebecca turned to her. "I apologize, I didn't mean any offense."

"It's okay," Katie said gently. "I would've probably thought the exact same thing in your shoes a few years ago. I saw the interview that your stepfather did and heard how he talked about you. My family background was pretty challenging, too. I didn't really believe there were good men in the world until I met Mark."

Rebecca didn't know what to make of that. She'd just met the woman, and yet there was something in her eyes that said maybe she actually did understand what it was like to grow up in a family like hers. What it was like to sit through awkward dinners, feeling the tension simmering through the air. How alone she'd felt.

She'd never really felt as though anyone had ever understood before. Not even Zack, who'd been disappointed back then that she'd never invited him to her house or introduced him to the General.

And yet Zack had still always known she'd needed him, even when she didn't know how to put it into words. He'd been there to protect her then. He'd been her safe place.

"Zack is the only truly good man I've known," she said.

"I know the feeling," Katie said. "I felt the same way when I met Mark."

"Zack and I are just friends," Rebecca added quickly. "Nothing more, and we haven't even seen each other in years."

"Zack's an interesting one." Katie nodded. "He's a hard guy to get to know in some ways. He's steady as a rock, reliable and easygoing. But he lets very few people into his inner circle. Zack helped saved my life once, and he's saved my husband's life more than once. I've never seen him as protective of anyone as he is of you."

Suddenly Katie's face paled. She dropped the clothes, gripped the back of the chair and took a deep breath in and out.

"You okay?" Rebecca asked.

"Braxton Hicks." Katie ran both hands over the sides of her belly and whispered a prayer under her breath. "The midwife calls them practice contractions. I've been having them on and off since yesterday. But I'm not due for six weeks yet."

Rebecca bent down and picked up the clothes. “Is there anything I can do?”

“No, I’m fine. I’m under strict instructions to avoid all stress—not that I’m meaning to imply you and Zack are stressful. We’d do anything for Zack.” Katie walked over to the desk. “I’m sorry if I threw you with what I said about your family. I think pregnancy has made me a bit blunt at times. But I’ve been following the news, and there was just something about General Miles’s demeanor that reminded me of both my stepfather and my sister’s husband. And not in a good way. So I read the blog and recognized a lot of the same patterns from what I lived through.”

Rebecca hugged the clothes to her chest and looked out at the sparkling light dancing on the surface of the lake.

“Seth told me that he wrote the blog,” she said. “I haven’t read it. I wasn’t sure I wanted to. Then I heard it was shut down.”

“I found a cached copy saved online,” Katie said. “You can read it on my computer, if you want to.”

“Will it upset me?”

“Probably. Yes. I imagine it will.” Katie’s hand brushed her shoulder. “But I’ll be around, so if you need someone to talk to, just shout.”

“Thank you.” The words seemed inadequate, but Rebecca didn't really know what else to say. Katie opened a website. Rebecca sat down and stared at the plain white screen with block black text:

The Truth About General Arthur Miles.

Rebecca's eyes scanned the page.

The website was laid out very simply. She'd expected some kind of flowery rhetoric, even some kind of rant. Instead, it was just a list of titles and links to documents that seemed to have been compiled in no specific order other than when the blog owner had found them.

There were copies of love letters the General had apparently exchanged with women around the world, some dating back decades, posted alongside X-rays of suspicious-looking injuries that Seth had sustained as a child—fractured collarbone, shattered wrist, bruising. There was a copy of the police report where a teenage Seth had apparently tried to report his mother missing, and a string of emails he'd sent to various officers begging them to open an investigation into her disappearance. Another was a letter from one of Seth's teachers from six months before the General married her mother, recommending Seth be removed from the home and placed in care, citing suspected neglect and the suspicion Seth was left home alone for days at a time.

Then she hit a letter that made the tears that had been silently building in her eyes spill and tumble onto the keyboard.

It was an email from her mother, sent to a very old email address she'd stopped checking years ago, after Seth had hacked her password:

Dear Becs,
I don't know if this is the right address to write to you at. I tried calling your phone but didn't get an answer. I'm guessing you're busy traveling and doing your video thing. I know you're mad I never told you anything about your real father. When I found out I was pregnant, I promised your father I'd never tell you the truth about him, because he was going to tell you himself when he was ready.

But now he's told me that he's falling in love with another woman, and having a child with her, and I don't think he's ever going to tell you.

General Arthur Miles is your real father. We met when he was married to Seth's mother and I was working as a waitress. We had a secret relationship for years and I'm not proud of that. I think Seth's mother knew. He kept promising he'd leave her. But then she had Seth and he stayed with her, and disappeared for a while.

Then when Seth's mother died he made good on his promise to take care of us. On the condition I was a good mother to Seth and never told anyone he was your dad.

I don't know what to do now. The General says that he can't divorce me because it'll be bad for his career. He wants me to agree to just leave him.

But I don't know how I'm going to live without him, either. I'm scared. He promised to take care of me. But he didn't...

The letter rambled on, growing more anxious and incoherent with every line, reminding her of just how sick her mother had been.

Now the tears were falling so hard from Rebecca's eyes that she couldn't see the words on the screen.

Seth's words from the night before flooded her memory.

Wake up, Becs! You're the only one who might even understand...I created that blog about our father... My father. Your father...I was trying to protect my sister...

Was this what Seth had been trying to tell her? That he was really her half brother? How long had he known? Since before her mother had married their father? Since he'd hacked into her account and found the email her mother had sent before she died?

Pain was building like a weight in her chest.

Her head dropped into her arms and she prayed. *Lord, this hurts so much I don't know how I'm ever going to handle it.*

Then firm, warm hands touched her shoulders. Rough lips brushed the top of her head.

Then she heard Zack's voice, comforting, strong. "It's okay, Becs. You're okay."

Zack stood behind her. She hadn't even heard him come in, but now here he was, dressed in green military fatigues, looking every bit the soldier, with his arms outstretched to comfort her. She stood up and almost tumbled into his arms. He held her. Tightly. Lifting her up off the ground and cradling her into his strength.

His lips brushed the tears from her face. His arms cradled her back.

"You're strong, Becs." Zack's voice filled with so much emotion that he almost choked. "You're stronger than this. I know it hurts so bad, and I hate that I can't somehow make the pain stop. But you're going to make it. You're the strongest, bravest person I know. I know who you are. I love who—"

An unusual ringing filled the air. He set her

down gently and pulled a large, clunky-looking phone from his belt.

The screen read Unknown Caller.

"Katie?" Zack called toward the hallway. "Okay if I answer this?"

No answer from Katie. The phone was still ringing.

Zack looked at Rebecca. "Sorry, I need to take this. It could be my commanding officer or Mark. I'll be back. Promise. Just give me a minute."

He stepped outside the front door, leaving her alone again.

Rebecca sank back into the chair, as if the air had been sucked from her lungs.

Her past was a lie. Her present had been stripped from her. And as she watched Zack's strong form stride away in his green fatigues, she knew she'd never have the future she dreamed of, either.

A future with the only man I've ever loved.

The computer beeped. She looked back at the screen. The website must have refreshed because now the blog was gone. Instead, red filled the screen under the word locked and a password prompt box. She hit the escape key, hoping to get back to the blog.

The screen read Incorrect Password.

And then up popped a second message, in

tiny letters, just for a fraction of a second, but long enough for her to read the words.

Hey, Becs. Really am sorry. Remember, you're a winner.

"So, inform the powers that be that I'm on my way in," Zack said, holding the phone to his ear. A breeze brushed his shoulders. His eyes rose to the canopy of green trees and endless blue sky. How long would he spend behind bars? Even when he was cleared, how long would he be grounded for? "I'm already in uniform, even. Just because that's all I've really got left that isn't ruined by the water. I'll go straight to base and check in. I should be there in about nine hours."

"I'm really sorry about this." Jeff's voice cracked in his ear. "I'll pull some strings to make sure there are no video or news cameras and that you've got a clear route in. Sorry I can't do more. I have faith the matter will be cleared up quickly. But I can't promise anything about your security clearance or your ability to stay with the task force. You were warned to stay away from Rebecca Miles and to extricate yourself from this entire situation."

Yeah, yeah, he was. But he'd been following his heart.

Lord, even now my heart feels like a lion roaring inside my chest. And I've prayed to You to help me tame it! Now it's tearing my life apart. And I don't know what to do.

He glanced back at the windows but saw nothing but his own reflection looking back.

"What's the update on Seth and Rebecca Miles?" Jeff asked.

"Seth Miles is still missing. Rebecca Miles is staying at the safe house for now. If there really is a leak inside our own military and Black Talon managed to infiltrate our police force, I'm going to advise her to stay hidden until I've spoken with officials who can guarantee her safe extraction and due process."

Thankfully, Mark's prototype phone would be untraceable.

"You realize that you're not doing yourself any favors if you walk in with demands?" Jeff said. "I strongly suggest you focus on one battle at a time."

He frowned. Rebecca had questioned whether or not he should even trust Jeff. The major had been Zack's only source of information, and had certainly known their movements well enough to send Black Talon right to them. Had Zack been wrong to trust a man he'd served with for years?

"Yes, sir. But I'm afraid it's nonnegotiable."

The phone beeped in Zack's hands. He glanced at the screen. There was an incoming call with a British area code.

"Hang on," Zack added. "I need a moment."

"Understood. Call me back."

The line went dead. Zack pushed the call-waiting button. "Hello?"

"Zack? That you?"

"Mark! Hey, man! What are you doing in Britain? Your beautiful wife told me you were in the Middle East."

"I'm in the air over Europe actually, en route to Heathrow," Mark said. "This little kerfuffle you've gotten yourself in made the international news. When I saw your name on the screen and heard you'd placed an emergency phone call, I caught the first plane out. I'm going to transfer in London and then head for home. Was just calling my wife to tell her I'll be there in about fifteen hours."

By which time Zack would be in custody. "Sorry, I'm not going to be able to meet you at the airport. But just got off the phone with my commanding officer. I'm heading to base to turn myself in."

"I'm sorry, man." Mark let out a long blow of breath. "That's pretty lousy. Guessing it's bad?"

"Code-red levels of bad."

"Got it," Mark said. Zack could hear the rumble of the airplane in the background. "This woman named Rebecca whose name was on the news with yours. She's the same one you used to talk about? The one you've always been in love with?"

The words hit Zack in the gut. It had been one thing to tell joking stories about the one perfect woman he'd known years ago. It was a whole different ball game dealing with her face-to-face.

"Same woman, yeah. You can ask Katie all about her. They've been bonding."

"Stay brave. Stay strong. You'll get through this." Mark was talking again. Zack couldn't tell if he was talking about facing arrest for treason, battling his feelings for Rebecca, or both. "If you could pass me over to my wife that'd be awesome."

"On my way." Zack started back into the house. "Congrats on the baby news by the way."

"Thanks." Mark laughed. "Took us by surprise. Katie's taking it all in stride better than I am."

"How's your family taking it?"

"Dad's thrilled. My sister, Sunny—the busy CEO—is still not really talking to me. But

Katie's doing her best to keep the lines of communication with her open."

Zack reached the living room. Rebecca was sitting at the computer. Katie was leaning over her shoulder. "Hey, Katie. It's your husband."

"Thanks." She took the phone and disappeared down the hallway.

"Everything okay?" Zack sat down beside Rebecca.

"No." She shook her head. "Seth locked the blog but he left me a message." Her fingers typed furiously, and Zack saw a series of asterisk stars. "Now look."

She hit Enter. The screen flashed.

Incorrect Password.

Hey, Becs. Really am sorry. Remember, you're a winner.

"He left me a clue. He expects me to crack it. But I don't know what it means."

"Can I help?" Zack asked.

"Absolutely, you can try. But knowing him, he'll have chosen something personal. Something he thinks nobody else will know. And I've tried everything I can think of."

"It's okay." He slid his chair over beside her. "You'll get this. I believe in you."

His fingers brushed the back of her neck. He could feel her tension dissolving under his fingertips. Her head fell into the palm of his hand, and for a moment he felt her hair slipping through his fingers.

Did she have any idea how much she affected him?

"I'm so sorry I brought you into all this," she said.

"Hey, none of this is your fault. I went looking for you, remember? I brought myself into this. What's more, I'm not even the least bit sorry I'm in it."

She turned her face toward his. His fingers brushed her cheek.

"But you could go to jail," she said.

"I could. But it's not the first set of bars I've ever been behind. At least this time I'll be in my home country, in a place that believes in courts, lawyers and due process. I'll be fine. I'll be straight with you. If I'm charged with anything, the charges will be secret. If I go to court, it'll be a classified court and if I'm incarcerated, you won't know where. But when I can and the dust clears, I'll get in touch and let you know I'm okay. I'm just sorry I won't get more time with you now. I'm sorry it took your stupid brother to give me the push I needed to contact you. Most of all, I'm sorry I didn't have the courage to take you to that sports banquet, way back when. I just couldn't believe you actually liked me."

"Zack." She whispered his name. His chest grew tighter, as if his heart had gotten too big to fit in his rib cage. He felt himself look away. But then her fingers brushed his jawline, pulling his face toward her, until his eyes were staring straight into hers. "Listen to me. You were the most amazing, incredible, gorgeous person I'd ever met. I more than liked you back then. I loved you."

The pressure in his chest grew, until it seemed to move up into his throat. He swallowed hard. "Well, I thought I'd fallen in love with you."

"Then you should've told me that," she said. "You should've apologized. You should've kissed me goodbye."

"I know," he murmured. He pulled her face closer. Her eyes closed. He felt her breath on his skin.

"You should've known you mattered more to me than any stupid trophy— Trophy!" Rebecca's eyes jerked open. She jumped back, ran for his bag and yanked out the broken base of the trophy. "'Technically Flawless.' Try that. 'Rebecca Miles, Technically Flawless.'"

He entered the words into the password box and hit Enter.

The box disappeared. Rebecca landed on the seat beside him.

A video feed filled the screen. It looked as if it was shot from a computer webcam. Seth was sitting alone at a computer facing the screen in a large empty room. There were colored blocks of peeling paint on the crumbling walls. Faded lines ran across the dirt-covered floor. A heavily tattooed man stood behind him. *Dmitry.*

He nudged Seth with the barrel of the gun. "What are you doing? Keep typing."

Seth faked a laugh. "You're asking us to revitalize a deactivated computer decryption program and set it up to take out eighteen separate targets around the world. Banks. Government sites. Technology and weapons companies. And you want it done by twelve noon. That's a pretty tall order."

Seth leaned back and stretched his hands over his head. Sun slanted through the dusty, cracked windows. There was some kind of tower outside. The lettering was faint.

"Only two people in the whole wide world have the power to pull off something of this level, you know that?" he said, as if he was talking to Dmitry. "Me and my little sister. Well, my half sister. You know how she found me? Online. She'd grown up in some horrible orphanage and all she wanted was proof that our father was really her father. But he refused to even talk to her. So she came and found me. We thought that together we could use her program to see if we could find what really happened to my mother, find out if we had other siblings and expose all of our father's lies. I did my best to help her. Unlimited power to unlock any password on the internet, eh? But it didn't quite go that way. Then again, I've never been much of a brother."

Seth nudged the screen further. Then she saw her. A young woman with pale blond hair, bound and gagged to the chair behind Seth.

Zack gasped. Rebecca grabbed Zack's hand.

"That's Maria Snow," Zack said, his voice grave. "She's the woman who created the decryption program, who I rescued from Eastern Europe a few months ago."

Tears were pushing into the corners of Rebecca's eyes.

"If Seth's right, she's also my little sister."

THIRTEEN

Zack held Rebecca's hand tightly and felt her body lean against his shoulder.

Maria's head lolled on her chest. She looked unconscious.

So, Maria had traded in her plea deal with the Canadian government, to try to prove her father's identity and contact Seth, then talked Seth into stealing the program she'd traded them for her life, and then ended up back in the clutches of the very people she'd fled to Canada to escape. Anger burned in his chest. As someone who'd lost both parents, he couldn't say he didn't understand the ache that had pushed her to do it. But that didn't mean he liked it.

Seth nudged the camera back to his face.

"You talk, I shoot her," a heavily accented voice barked. "You move, I shoot her. You do anything, I shoot her."

Seth's eyes flickered to the screen.

"Sorry, Becs. Guess I messed this up pretty bad. Goodbye."

He touched a key. The screen went black. The password screen popped up again. Zack quickly retyped the password. The video restarted from the beginning.

"It's not a live video feed," Rebecca said quietly. She leaned her elbows on the desk. "He used the computer's webcam to record a quick video message and uploaded it for me. He wanted me to know they had him and Maria, that Maria was my half sister, and that whatever havoc came because of what her decryption program did, they were doing it under duress. He wanted to say goodbye before they killed him."

He couldn't imagine how she was feeling, suddenly discovering she had two half siblings, both fathered by General Miles, who were now in the clutches of criminals who were going to kill them. What's worse was he knew there was nothing he could do about it.

Zack leaned back and crossed his arms. "I'm going to have to call it in, but really we've got no information. We don't know what the targets are, where they're being held or even when this video was made."

"We can't answer the first question, but we

can answer the second two." She leaned past him, pulled up a list of computer programs.

"What are you doing?"

"Looking for a video-editing program." She selected one. The program opened. Moments later the video opened up inside the new window. Her fingers were typing so fast he could barely keep up. Her lips quivered and he could see where tears had been glistening in her eyes moments before, but her hands were steady. She pulled up an audio mixer and played with sliding levels. "Based on background noise, they're somewhere pretty isolated. I can hear some footsteps outside on what sounds like concrete. But no road traffic, city noise or electricity humming. My best guess is there are five or six people guarding an old building, somewhere that's not near a main road."

"You can tell all that from that tiny bit of video?"

"Oh, you'd be amazed at what I can tell from video." She flipped back to the video and zoomed in on the window, then she adjusted the colors until shadows appeared. "The glass on the window is cracked, but not broken. So the place is abandoned but not vandalized. There are stripes on the floor, a water tower outside the window—" She sat back, and exhaled so sharply it was as if she'd just been socked in the gut. "They're in our old gym, at our old high school, on our old base at Remi Lake. But I thought they closed that place down decades ago."

"They decommissioned the base," Zack said. "And they sold the land to a communications company who set up a huge telecommunication array there. But some of the old buildings are still standing."

"According to the hidden time stamp, the video was uploaded to the website seventy-two minutes ago," Rebecca said, "which means if he's telling the truth we have a little over thirty-four minutes before he's supposed to release the virus."

He leaned back. His eyes scanned Seth's eyes through the screen. "Do you believe he's telling the truth this time?"

She nodded. "I do."

"Okay." He stood up. "I'm going to call Jeff and tell him everything I know."

Her hand grabbed his. "Are you sure we can trust him?"

"We need to trust somebody," he said, "and yes, I trust Jeff. I just hope he can get somebody deployed to the old base in time."

"And if they can't?" she asked.

Zack ran his hand over his eyes. He'd risked his life on a rather dangerous military mission to pluck Maria from danger and she'd thrown it all away to team up with Seth. Now they had to rescue her again?

And what about Seth?

For a moment all Zack could see was the inside of his own palm. Then he pictured himself standing back on the mats. Feeling overweight and alone.

Shaking. Angry. Humiliated.

Hurting. Hating Seth with every fiber of his being.

Lord, what would You do? What should I do?

He knew the answer before he'd even finished breathing the prayer.

"Then I'm going to save them." He dropped his hand from his face and looked at Rebecca. "Both of them. If the military can't get there in time, I'll go in after them. I'm not going to let them die without a fight."

Then he ran toward the bedroom door. "Katie? You there? I need your encrypted phone back and I've got to borrow a vehicle."

Katie appeared in the hallway. Her face was pale.

"Everything okay?" she asked.

"No." Rebecca crossed the floor toward her. "My brother and a woman he says is my sister are being held captive at gunpoint and they're going to unlock a bunch of highly sensitive financial and government websites, within the hour."

Zack dialed Jeff Lyons. It rang twice. Then a click.

"Hello?"

"Major Lyons, it's Sergeant Keats. I've received new intel that both Seth Miles and Maria Snow are being held at the decommissioned Remi Lake military base." He looked up. Rebecca and Katie were already heading for the door. "They're being held by members of Black Talon who've given them thirty minutes to simultaneously unlock eighteen different government, military and financial institutions. I'm sorry, I don't know the exact targets for the decryption."

"How do you know this?" Jeff asked.

"Seth planted a video on his blog for his sister. The password is 'Rebecca Miles comma Technically Flawless.'" Zack slung his bag over this shoulder and grabbed Katie's rifle. "I'm on my way to the Remi Lake base now."

"Stand down. We'll assemble a team and get them out to Remi."

"There isn't time." The door swung shut behind him. "Tell me straight, do I really have a warrant out for my arrest?"

"No, I've just been able to confirm that there

isn't a warrant out for your arrest or for Rebecca Miles's," Jeff said. "Although you're both wanted for questioning, obviously. But somebody leaked false information to the press, including the claim of a warrant. Just one of a whole bunch of leaks we're trying to stem here."

Zack's feet ran down the path toward the boat, hoping that Jeff was telling the truth and they weren't going to be arrested by the first cop they passed.

"There's going to be a huge investigation into this whole mess when it's done," Jeff added. "For now, just stay low, come back to base and let the higher-ups coordinate an actual mission."

"I'm afraid I can't do that." Zack reached the dock. Rebecca and Katie were already in the boat. Rebecca was in the driver's seat. He covered the phone with his hand for a moment, glanced at Rebecca and said, "You two wait here. I'm going alone."

"No, we're going." She cut her eyes at Katie, who was gripping a life jacket so hard it was as if she was trying to pop it.

What else was he missing? Whatever it was, there wasn't time to fight two battles at once. Zack jumped in the motorboat and yanked off the mooring ropes. Rebecca started the motor.

"Jeff." His attention snapped back to the phone. "Maria Snow was my mission. I got her back to Canada safely and now she's in Black Talon hands."

"She's not your mission anymore," the major said. "She's now on Canadian soil. This is an RCMP matter now. You know as well as I do, you can't save every target. Zack, as your friend I'm giving it to you straight. You're making a big mistake. You're letting your emotions cloud your judgment. You're throwing your career away over some girl you haven't seen in years."

Yup. Maybe he was. Zack sat back and watched the wake spreading behind them. "Can you guarantee me that a team will reach the base in time to extract Seth and Maria in the next twenty-eight minutes?"

"You know I can't do that."

They reached the dock. Rebecca cut the engine. Zack leaped out and tied the boat down. Rebecca tossed him the keys. They ran for the garage and Katie's black SUV. To his surprise, Rebecca got into the back with Katie.

"Tell you what." Zack climbed into the driver's seat. "I'll get there, recon the situation and wait for backup. I will only take action if the hostages are in immediate danger and the team doesn't make it in time."

"Sergeant, if you ignore a direct order ordering you back to base, you will face a court-martial."

"I know." Zack started the engine. "So, I'm praying really hard you aren't going to order me back to base."

"Would it make any difference if I did?" Jeff asked.

Zack put the truck into gear. His eyes glanced at the clock. Twenty-seven minutes left. "I'm not going to answer that question. But I am going to have to hang up soon, because there's a law against talking on a cell phone while driving." The major snorted. "But if it's any help, tell whoever's breathing down your neck right now that I'm the only soldier trained in counterterrorism and special ops our military has in the area of an imminent international terrorist plot."

The line went dead. Zack put the vehicle in gear. The vehicle peeled off into the woods.

"Just to warn you, I'm going to have to speed a bit if we have any hope of getting there in time to save Seth and Maria," Zack said. "Good news is that Jeff Lyons is an excellent CO and will make sure to throw everything he's got at getting people to that base and getting them out alive. Bad news, they might not make it in time." No answer. He glanced at the rearview mirror. Katie was leaning against Rebecca's shoulder. Rebecca was gripping both her hands tightly. Then Katie let go and sat back against the seat. "What don't I know?"

"Katie keeps having contractions," Rebecca said. "And they've been getting steadily worse. We don't know if it's a false alarm or if something's actually wrong with the baby. But either way we can't just leave her stranded alone on the island and take her only mode of transportation. She should really head to a hospital."

So that's why Rebecca had been so insistent about Katie coming with them.

Okay, Lord, now what? The hospital was over an hour's drive away.

"You're not going to worry," Rebecca said, firmly. "Either of you. We're going to stay calm. The contractions will stop. Zack will get to the base. Then we'll get to the hospital. It's all going to be okay."

Zack's hands held steady on the steering wheel. How was he even going to disarm at least six foreign terrorists? Katie's hunting rifle and his pocket knife weren't much in terms of weapons. Trees flew past. He edged the accelerator. With every breath, he waited for the phone to ring with a direct order commanding him back to base. It didn't ring.

"Zack?" It was Katie. "Can I have the phone?"

"Absolutely." He passed it back. He could hear her praying as she dialed.

They passed the faded sign for the former base. Then he could see the remains of the outer fence. He pulled in beside the empty guard post. The road was deserted. Katie was pushing buttons on the phone, as if she was dealing with an automated system. He leaned back between the seats and handed Rebecca the rifle. She hesitated, then took it.

"I'll be back as quickly as I can." He grabbed her other hand. "If I don't make it back—"

"Don't." She squeezed his hand so tightly his fingers ached, but he didn't let go. "Don't say goodbye. Just go and come back. Okay? I believe in you. I trust you."

He took a deep breath. "Okay."

She dropped his hand. He got out of the truck and jogged down the faded, cracked pavement where he used to run with Rebecca. The base was deserted. He weaved through the empty buildings, staying tight to the walls, keeping out of sight. He looked at his watch. Just eight minutes left. Then he saw the crumbling facade of their old high school. Two large vans were parked outside the door. A man in black fatigues stood by the entrance to the courtyard, clutching a Springfield XD(M) semiautomatic.

Zack crept around the side of the building,

just outside his line of sight, and coughed. The large man ran around the corner and straight into Zack's fist. He crumpled to the ground. *That's one down.* Zack relieved him of his weapon, then bound his hands with the man's own belt and gagged him with his own handkerchief. He left him unconscious by the remnants of a concrete garbage shed. Not ideal, but he didn't have a lot of time. He crossed through the school courtyard where he'd stood in the rain as a teenager and said his last said goodbye to Rebecca. Grass poked through the crumbling cement. Not another person in sight. He stepped in the school's back door and nearly bumped noses with a man leaning against the wall.

Zack knocked him out, bound his hands, gagged him and left him in a supply closet. *That's two.* Just how many more of them were there? He kept going toward the gym and found a third man just outside the gym door.

This one was barely older than sixteen and looked so twitchy and frightened, Zack's heart ached. He had a freshly inked Black Talon tattoo on his neck, but no name overtop. This man was such a new recruit he hadn't even had a first kill. Hopefully, he never would. The young man raised his weapon. In a swift, severe motion, Zack twisted it from his hands and pointed it back at the kid's face. The boy's hands shot up.

"I don't want to hurt you. I just need to find the hostages. A man and a woman. Now, nod to show you understand me."

The boy nodded.

"Are they in that room?" He tilted his head toward the gym.

More nodding.

"How many guards are in there with him?"

The boy shook his head.

"What do you mean, no? Are you saying there are no guards in there with him? Zero guards? You're guarding him alone?"

The boy's head shook then nodded, panicked. His fingers formed a zero.

It made no sense. On the video, Dmitry had been the one guarding Seth.

Yet the boy looked absolutely petrified.

"All right," Zack said. "I'm not going to hurt you. But I am going to tie you up, okay?"

The boy swallowed hard. Then he turned on his heel and raced down the hallway. Zack leveled the barrel of his weapon at the boy's back. Then he lowered his sights and let the boy go.

Zack slipped into the gym. Maria sat slumped in a chair, her hands still bound, her head flopped against her chest. Seth sat alone at a folding table in the center of the room. His hands weren't bound. His legs weren't bound. He was just sitting alone, beside a laptop computer, which was attached to a larger desktop computer by what looked like a mass of cables.

Seth glanced up. His lip was bloody. His eye was bruised. "Zack. You found us."

"I did. Rebecca found your video and used it to figure out where you were." Zack inched his way across the room, checking every corner as he did. "You okay if I go check on Maria?"

"Yeah, please," Seth said. "I think she's okay. They drugged her because she started screaming, so they left me to do the programming on my own."

Zack crossed over to her. She was still breathing and her pulse was strong. He carefully slit the rope off her wrists and cut the gag from her mouth. The desktop computer beeped. Zack looked up. A box popped up on the desktop computer's screen. Seth typed: Reset Timer. The box disappeared.

"So, you about ready to go?" Zack asked, cautiously. "Rebecca's here, just outside waiting to see you."

"I'm afraid I can't do that. See, the decryptions have all been set to go on the laptop." Seth nodded to the smaller computer. "All I have to do is let the counter on the desktop here get down to zero and it will go off. *Bam.*

Eighteen international sites, all simultaneously unlocked, for Black Talon to plunder at will. Unless somebody like me goes back in and resets all the passwords, and they don't want that to happen."

Seth leaned back and pointed under the table and Zack saw what was keeping him there.

C4 explosives. Enough to take down the whole building.

"See, it works like this," Seth said. "The moment the decryption starts on the laptop, and those sites become live, the big computer detonates the bomb and our old high school goes up in flames."

The computer beeped. Seth reset the timer. No wonder so few people were guarding the building. They'd only left those they thought were disposable. A motor rumbled in the air outside. A helicopter was approaching.

"Is that our rescue?" Seth asked.

"I don't know," Zack said. He set his knife on the table. It was definitely a copter. But only one. And it didn't sound military. "Can you stop the bomb?"

"I might be able to electronically disconnect the two machines so that the timer no longer acts as a detonator and the decryption program is no longer connected to the explosions. But not while I have to keep resetting the timer."

Seth's eyes met Zack's. His old bully looked exhausted, broken. "I'm pretty sure that kid on the door was supposed to have shot me by now, first kill and all, but he was still getting up the courage."

Then he glanced at Maria. "I'm really sorry, Zack. You're probably every bit as wonderful as Rebecca thinks you are. But I can't risk you taking Maria to safety and leaving me here to die."

Seth jumped up, threw Maria over his shoulder and ran.

FOURTEEN

Rebecca kept one arm firmly around Katie's shoulders and her other hand on the rifle as they ran for the base's helicopter pad. The white-and-gold corporate helicopter of Mark's sister's company, Shields Construction, descended slowly from the sky toward them.

Katie pressed her lips together hard and squeezed Rebecca's free hand with both of hers. Her face was so white, Rebecca worried that Katie was going to pass out unless she managed to distract her from the pain.

"Tell me something," Rebecca shouted over the roar of the motor. "If being a journalist wasn't your dream, what was your dream?"

"To make a difference," Katie shouted. "To change lives. To help people. I don't know if I could've put it into words back then. I just knew I wanted to be a force for good in the world."

The contraction stopped.

"And you?" Katie asked. "What's your dream?"

Rebecca looked from the helicopter to the remains of the base that had once meant so much pain. She'd thought it was to be free. Free to go wherever she wanted, to be able to do whatever she wanted to. She'd wanted to finally feel free from the life she'd lived twenty years ago.

Maybe what I really wanted was to finally be free from always reliving the memories.

"I don't know," Rebecca said. "Maybe I don't have one. Maybe it's traveling to new places and telling new stories with my camera. Creating new memories."

"Sounds like a pretty good dream to me."

The helicopter landed. Rebecca blinked. A stunning young woman with long raven-black hair was behind the controls. Katie waved to her.

"Rebecca Miles, meet my sister-in-law," Katie shouted. "This is Sunny Shields, CEO of Shields Construction. Sunny, this is Rebecca."

A young man in a crisp suit opened the door and reached for Katie's hand.

"Nice to meet you," Sunny called. She waved at Katie. "So, you ready to go?"

"Absolutely, just give me a second."

Rebecca set the rifle down at her feet and hugged Katie goodbye. "Stay safe."

"I'm guessing I can't convince you to come with me?"

Rebecca glanced back at the high school. "I'm staying."

The young man helped Katie into the helicopter.

"Wait! Hey!" Seth shot around the corner of the building, carrying Maria over his shoulder. "Wait for us! She needs to get to a hospital!"

Her brother pelted across the ground and bolted for the helicopter.

"Let Albright take her," Sunny yelled, as the young man leaped from the back of the helicopter and ran toward Seth. "He's trained as a paramedic."

Albright took Maria from Seth's arms and carried her into the helicopter.

Rebecca grabbed Seth's arm. "Wait, where's Zack?"

"Don't worry about him!" Seth shouted. "We've got to go! The building's going to explode."

Seth tried to pull away. But she refused to let go.

"The building's going to explode and you just left Zack in there to explode with it? Do you know how to stop the bomb?" Seth looked down. *So, that would be a yes.* "We're going back in there to save him!"

The helicopter rotors thrummed above them. Sunny was yelling that they had to go. Seth yanked his arm away. Rebecca glanced toward the helicopter.

Then she felt the cold metal barrel of the hunting rifle pressed into her neck. She turned.

"I'm really sorry to do this to you, Rebecca," Seth said, the rifle shaking in his hands, "but we're both going to get into that helicopter and leave. I don't want to die here and I don't want you to die here, either. I don't know for sure I can stop the bomb. I can only try. But even if I can, I'd rather die than end up in military prison, spending the rest of my life behind bars at the mercy of people like the General."

"Not everyone in uniform is like our father, Seth. A whole lot of them are good and decent, like Zack."

She didn't even look at the metal pressed against her skin. Instead she looked at her brother.

"But I understand why you want to run." Tears filled her eyes. "I get why you're afraid. I'm sorry I never did before, but I do now. I read your blog, Seth. I know that your father hurt you. I know that you're my half brother and Maria is our half sister, and that the only reason you did all this was because you wanted to use the decryption program to expose him for who he was, and help Maria prove she was his daughter, and find out what happened to your mother."

"Nobody gets it." Angry tears were building in Seth's eyes. "Nobody ever has."

"Well, I do," she said. "I might be only one person, but I do. I didn't get it before, and don't get me wrong, I still think you were a rotten brother and I still think you deserve to go to jail for stealing that program. But I get why you did it. And I forgive you."

The computer beeped. Zack typed, Reset Timer.

Then he swung around to face a skinny thug who'd just run into the gym.

The Black Talon opened fire. *AK-47. Sloppy.* Zack ducked under the bullet and caught the man in the chest. The gun fell to the floor.

Then a fresh spray of bullets filled the air as Dmitry ran into the room.

Welcome. Coming to check how your hostages escaped and why your bomb hasn't gone off?

Zack rolled. Then kicked straight up, knocking the gun from Dmitry's hands.

The computer beeped.

Zack turned on his heel and ran for the computer. The counter was counting down. Zack typed, Reset Timer.

A gun barrel clicked behind him.

"Hands up." Dmitry had recovered faster than Zack had expected. Zack raised his hands. "Now. You stand up, slowly."

Zack leaped to his feet and grabbed for the gun. It fired into the air. Plaster fell down from the ceiling. Zack wrenched the weapon from Dmitry's hands and leveled a blow to his face. Dmitry grunted and fell to the floor. His skinny buddy was passed out cold. There was a clatter of footsteps running down the hallway. Zack spun toward the door and raised his weapon to fire.

The computer beeped again.

Rebecca ran through the door. Seth was one step behind her.

"What are you two doing here?"

"Helping." Her hand brushed his arm as she ran past him to the computer.

Vehicles were screeching to a stop outside. Voices were shouting. Still, none of it sounded anything like the kind of backup he was hoping for.

Zack kept his gun trained on the door. Dmitry was glaring at him, but not moving. "Where's Maria?"

"Woman named Sunny picked Katie and

Maria up in the helicopter," Rebecca said. "Said she'd take them both to the hospital."

Thank You, God. "You should've gone with them."

"No, I shouldn't." Rebecca slid into the chair. "If you're going to blow up here in this stupid gym, I'm going with you." Then she looked up at Seth. "How do we do this?"

"You keep resetting the timer every time the computer beeps," Seth said. "I'll electronically disconnect the timer from the bomb."

An eruption of gunfire sounded from the hallway. Then there was a lot more shouting. None of it was in English.

"Hate to break it to you," Zack shouted, "but I think things just got messier. It sounds like more Black Talons just showed up and they're not big fans of the ones already here."

A head popped through the doorway. Then huge tattooed arms bulging out of a bulletproof vest.

"Stop typing!" The bulletproofed Black Talon shouted. "Now! Or I'll shoot!"

Seth kept typing. "Presume you got this covered, Zack?"

"Yup." He more than had it covered. That vest might keep Zack from killing him, but he'd still feel the impact. Zack fired, his bullets hitting the man square in the chest. Behind him he could hear fierce typing. The computer beeped a single long, drawn-out beep.

"Got it!" Seth yanked the laptop away from the larger tangle of machines and wires. He stood up. "Now, all I've got to do is shut down all eighteen decryption sites one by one, before Black Talon robs a bank or sets off some nuclear weapons."

Dmitry leaped to his feet. Zack decked him in the jaw. He fell back down. "Any chance you can deactivate the decryption while we run?"

"Absolutely." Seth grabbed the laptop and stood up.

"Great." Zack looked at Rebecca. "How did you get Seth to come with you?"

"I told him I believed him and when all this was done, I'd do what I could to continue his search for his mother and any other half siblings we might have, and prove Maria's really our sister."

Zack nodded. That would be a pretty tall order and one he probably couldn't be a part of. But right now, all they could do was fight the battle in front of them.

"Did you ever learn to shoot?" he asked.

"I've always known how to shoot." She grinned. "What I did was learn how to aim."

"Don't shoot except in self-defense, okay?"

He grabbed a Glock off Dmitry's limp body and handed it to her.

"You've got it." Damp hair fell over her face. Her eyes glistened.

He'd never loved anything as much as he loved her right now.

"Do whatever you've got to do, Zack," she added. "Give me whatever orders you need to give me, and I'll follow them. You'll get us out of here, alive. I trust you."

Zack took a deep breath, and felt calm as clear air entered his lungs. His pulse slowed. He had this. They ran down the hallway single file. A firefight had erupted in the old cafeteria between two warring groups of Black Talons. He clipped one thug who was firing from the landing by the science lab. Then he led them down into the basement and wove through the old locker hallways, and finally up the back stairway by the parking lot. There was the roar of rotors above. They looked up. A fleet of military helicopters was descending from the sky. Police vehicles swarmed up the driveway. *Thank You, God.*

Seth ran toward the vehicles and raised his hands above his head, still clutching the laptop. "I'm Seth Miles! I'm surrendering! But I'm also busy defusing the decryption program hub by hub. I'm down to the last four.

So don't take the laptop away unless you know advanced programming."

He disappeared into the crowd of officers.

Zack ran to the nearest officer and briefed her on the situation inside the building. But as the authorities mobilized to surround the building, Zack took Rebecca by the hand and quickly led her down the road through the maze of oncoming vehicles, back to where they'd parked Katie's SUV. All four of Katie's tires had been shot out, no doubt by the second batch of Black Talons as they'd arrived. But thankfully his green bag was still under the front seat. He pulled it out, then turned to face Rebecca.

"You've got to get out of here," he said. "The situation's going to get really violent and pretty nasty and there's still a chance someone could set off the bomb inside the building. This is no place for civilians. I'll try to find someone I know and trust to take you in. The good news is that it looks like there's no warrant out for your arrest, at least according to Jeff, but you're still going to be wanted for questioning." He dropped the bag by his feet and pulled her into his arms. "But right now, I'm just glad we got a chance to finally say a real goodbye."

"And then what happens with you?" She looked up at him.

"Well, despite the fact I'm in fatigues, I'm still not on active duty," he said. "I'm going to report in for duty and hopefully catch a ride back to base. If all goes well, this will be sorted out quickly with my superiors. I never actually disobeyed a direct order, so I shouldn't face disciplinary action, especially as Seth turned himself in, Maria is safe, the decryption program has been found and our police are currently taking down a pretty large foreign terrorist cell. Hopefully, I'll still be able to be deployed overseas with my unit, this week."

"Then you'll disappear off the grid, to another undisclosed location, for an indefinite amount of time," Rebecca said.

There was a question in her eyes. A question he didn't know how to answer.

"Yes, I will. That's exactly what I'll do." He shook his head. "I don't know what you want me to say, Becs. Do you think I won't miss you? Do you think I want to say goodbye to you? Do you think I haven't lain awake at night over the past twenty years and wished I had you to come home to? But you know who I am, and you know what my job is. I'm a sergeant in the Armed Forces. I'm not going to take a desk job while I'm still young enough and strong enough to be out in the world fighting the battles that need to be fought."

Her shoulders rose and fell, and it felt as if a sigh had moved through her body into his.

"I never once told you I wanted you to give up a life in the military," she said. "Not once. I'm *proud* of you, Zack. I'm proud of what you do."

"Okay, well, I don't want you to spend your life sitting around waiting for me to come home," he said. "I don't want you to be unhappy. I don't want you to have to go through life feeling like every minute of every day the person you care about most is far away and out of reach. I *know* that feeling. I *lived* that feeling. That's how I felt about you every day, watching you across the gym. I felt that pain every day for weeks and months and years after we said goodbye. You were the slowest-closing wound I ever felt."

"But you were wrong." She pulled away. "I wasn't out of reach. I loved you, Zack. I wanted to be with you. But you didn't love who you were, so you pushed me away without even giving me a chance to try to be with you." Her arms crossed in front of her chest. "Just like you're pushing me away now."

He opened his mouth, but the blare of a horn froze his words on his lips. He looked up over the top of Rebecca's head. A beautiful black luxury truck was pulling down the driveway.

It stopped. An elderly man got out, in full military uniform, with trimmed white hair and a smart white moustache. Zack let go of Rebecca and snapped to attention. Every inch of his body pulled up with the same sign of respect he'd shown men and women superiors for the past twenty years.

"At ease, Sergeant," a voice boomed. "It is Sergeant Zachary Keats I assume?"

Rebecca gasped. Her face grew pale before she'd even turned to see who was now standing behind her.

"Yes sir," Zack said. "It's an honor to finally meet you, General Miles."

FIFTEEN

"Rebecca!" the General's voice sounded. "What a pleasure it is to see you again."

She turned slowly to face her stepfather, like someone trapped in a nightmare they couldn't wake up from, as every word and image from Seth's blog slowly filtered through her mind. She watched as he shook Zack's hand. Then his hand reached out to shake hers. She let him take it, feeling the tension rippling up her arm and into her shoulder, as his hand clasped hers.

You hurt my mother. You hurt Seth. You fathered a brilliant young woman on the other side of the ocean, who ended up in an orphanage and in the hands of Black Talon. And you denied her existence just like you tried to deny mine. And now, because being a rotten husband and father isn't a crime and nobody can prove how badly you treated my brother, you're going to get away with it, and become a senator.

She opened her mouth, but no words came out, as she realized in that moment that she was no longer afraid of the imposing man who'd walked into her life at thirteen and taken it over. She was very, very angry.

But Zack had both saluted him and stood at attention at his approach. Even at ease, Zack's shoulders were high and his back was straight, and she realized that for the first time she was truly seeing him as what he was—a soldier facing a superior officer.

"What are you doing here, sir?" Zack asked. His tone was deferential and there was a very slight nod to his head as he spoke.

"I heard about the military operation and that Rebecca was involved." General Miles folded his arms. "This whole situation has been quite upsetting, to say the least. Thankfully, I just got word that my son is safe and with police. But I wanted to make sure Rebecca was all right."

So, he'd come for Seth, but since Seth was with police he would settle for her? Or had he come to make sure all his wayward children were under control?

The General had waved a hand in the direction of the nearest group of uniformed men. Three ran over, with that steady gait that practically blared respect. The General led them over to the back of the truck and was instructing them to get something down.

It was only then that she saw the motorcycle—the General's vintage Triumph from World War Two. The same one Zack had admired through the window of their garage as a teenager. The one that Seth hadn't even dared touch. The General clasped a firm hand on Zack's shoulder. "I heard through the grapevine that you were a motorcycle enthusiast."

"Yes, sir." Zack's eyes scanned the bike as if it was a fresh puzzle to solve.

But Rebecca knew instantly what it was doing here.

"Consider this a little thank-you gift." The General steered Zack toward the bike. "I'm too old for a toy like this. It's about time it was passed down to someone who could appreciate its history and tradition."

"A gift." Zack's words were stilted. "That's beyond generous, sir."

A bribe. The General was actually trying to bribe Zack for his silence and cooperation. Like he'd probably bribed people all his life to keep his secrets.

"A token," the General said, "in gratitude for all you've done in the past twenty-four hours to resolve this situation swiftly. I've heard great things about you, soldier, and will be watching your career closely. I trust I'll be pleased with what I'll be seeing from you in the future." Then he turned to Rebecca. "Now, if you'd like to say your goodbyes to the good sergeant, I think it's time I take you home."

"Home?" Rebecca's voice sounded so strained it was like a rubber band ready to snap. The camper that had been her home was now lost, washed down to the bottom of a river.

"Sorry, I meant my home, in Ottawa." The General smiled. He turned to Zack. "You see, my wife and I have a small guesthouse in the back. We would be happy to help Rebecca find her feet."

"No, thank you." Rebecca crossed her arms, mirroring his. "I appreciate your very kind offer. But I'll be fine."

The General frowned.

"Rebecca." Zack's hand landed on her shoulder. His voice was firm, with a ring of authority she'd never heard before. "I think it's a wonderful thing that General Miles has offered to give you a ride back to his home in Ottawa. I hope you agree. Trust me. This could be a once-in-a-lifetime opportunity for you."

He picked up the faded green bag and slid it over her shoulder. Then Zack turned to the General. "Rebecca is the strongest person I know. She's been through a lot, and I think her greatest challenges are lying ahead. But trust me, she's got this."

She looked down at the faded, worn fabric, holding the few supplies they'd saved from her camper as it was sinking. She took a deep breath and looked up into Zack's face. The smile on Zack's face was as easygoing as it had always been. "You sure about this, Zack?"

You honestly think I should be going back to the home of this monster in sheep's clothing?

His eyes met hers, his gaze steady as steel. Then he took her hand and pressed it firmly against the bag, so she could feel the hard, smooth edge of her tiny video recorder inside. "Absolutely, trust me. This mission is all yours."

"Okay, I trust you." She leaned forward. Her lips slid across his cheek.

His hand brushed the base of her spine. "I'll have your back."

She turned and followed the General to his truck, feeling her heart beat with every move. *Zack, I hope you know what you're doing.*

A man in fatigues materialized to open the passenger door. She got in. The door shut firmly. The door lock clicked. The General pulled out onto the road. His lips pressed together in a straight line. The vehicle filled with the same cold, resentful silence she'd felt emanating from him since the first day she'd walked into his home. They reached a rural highway. Endless trees blurred past them. The empty road lay behind them.

"When we get to Ottawa, you'll meet with my lawyer and sign a nondisclosure agreement," the General said, without even looking at her. "You will then enter a ninety-day treatment program, at my expense and at a facility of my choosing. When you complete the program successfully, I'll give you a monthly stipend allowance, based on certain criteria being met."

So now he was going to pay her off, too. Like he'd tried to pay off her mother.

"I've never actually used drugs or alcohol," she said. "But you probably don't even care about that and just figured this would be a handy way of getting rid of me. You can probably find a facility that won't care, either, as long as you pay the bills."

He didn't even flinch and just continued talking as if she hadn't even spoken.

"You will not speak to members of the media or others without clearance. Ever. That includes any discussion of my family—"

"You mean *our* family," she cut him off. "Because according to my mother, you are my biological father, and I don't doubt that's the truth. I'm thinking you didn't care about her at all, until Seth's mother was gone and social services was threatening to take Seth from your home for abuse and neglect, so you quickly married my mother so that it would look like Seth had a stable home life and to keep your reputation intact. But by then you'd already terrorized Seth so badly he grew up to hate you and found his own way to fight back. Until finally he met our half sister Maria who created the decryption program he could use to expose you. I can't imagine how frightened you must have been, discovering some child you'd fathered in Europe, who'd been abandoned to an orphanage, was in Canada talking to Seth."

Again, the General didn't answer. He just gripped the steering wheel with huge pale hands. The highway was still empty behind her. Prayers poured silently through her heart. Her fingers brushed the green bag Zack had handed her. She could feel the tiny video camera she'd salvaged from her camper whirring quietly, recording nothing but a man driving in silence. Why did Zack think she could do this? She'd never been good at knowing the right words to say. Seth had been the one able to bait people into saying things. Not her. And the silent treatment had always been their father's weapon of choice.

"Seth is never going to stop fighting you," she said. Maybe she wouldn't get the confession she needed. Maybe all of this was for nothing and she wouldn't be able to stop him. But at least, for once, someone would be standing up to him. "Because his mother is gone and he'll never stop looking for her, or for other siblings like Maria scattered around the world in all the places you traveled."

His jaw clenched. "You will never speak to my son again."

"My brother!" She could feel her voice growing stronger. "Whether you like it or not, Seth is my brother, and I'm not going to turn my back on him, no matter how much you try to bribe me, like you tried to bribe my mother. I'll be doing everything in my power to help him and Maria expose who you are to the world. A man who bullied the women who loved him, disowned the children he made, who hurt the son who looked up to him, all while hiding behind a uniform he had no right wearing."

His hand flew into her face, so quickly the slap caught her in the jaw and knocked her head back against the seat. Then he reached into his jacket and pulled out a handgun. He placed it on his lap, one hand gripping the butt.

"We can do this the easy way or the hard way," he said, "but you will do what you are told, exactly as you're told, or you will die, and trust me, your body will never be found. Just like Seth will never find his mother's body, no matter how hard and long he looks for her. I have friends, and my friends will take care of you. They've taken care of more than one problem for me, and I have no problem adding you to that list. I don't tolerate failures."

Pain filled her head. Stars filled her eyes. Clarity filled her mind as Seth's words echoed in her memory.

He sent criminals after my sister!

"By friends, you mean Black Talon, don't you?" She pressed her lips together and tasted blood. "You're the military leak who's been supplying a foreign criminal group with weapons and supplies. Not because you believed in their cause. But because you needed someone to do your dirty work, like taking care of Seth's mother and Maria. You're the one who helped them get into the country illegally and who fed them the information they needed to find and capture Maria, and intercept her communications with Seth. He was right about you. You are a monster."

The General swung to slap her again. But this time she was ready. Her hand shot up, blocking his blow. Her other hand smashed him hard in the face. The truck swerved wildly. Her seat belt snapped her back against the seat. The truck swerved again, then screeched to a stop.

The General grabbed the gun and aimed it at her face with one hand. With the other he grabbed his cell phone, pushed a button and barked an order in what sounded like Russian. He hung up without even waiting for an answer.

"Now you've done it." His hands shook with rage. "My friends are coming. They will take you away and dispose of you. Like they've disposed of every other woman who thought she could defy me."

Her eyes rose to the rearview mirror. There was a small speck on the horizon. Someone was coming. "Not if my friend gets to you first."

"You think Sergeant Keats is coming to save you?" He laughed.

"Zack's an excellent soldier, who believes in everything you should've stood for, and that's exactly why he's the man to take you down."

The speck in the distance grew larger. She could hear the roar of the motor.

The General laughed. It was an ugly, angry sound. "You think I'd have lasted this long if I was that big a fool? That I didn't test his loyalty, like I've tested everyone else's? That bike's brakes don't work. I made sure of it. If he tries to come after you, he will crash and he will die, and I'll have one less person to worry about."

He turned the key in the ignition again. But the truck wouldn't move. He swore. The motorcycle grew louder. She could see it in the side mirror now. Shining against the shimmering blacktop. She grabbed for the gun with both hands and tried to yank it from the General's grasp. It went off. The passenger window behind her shattered in a spray of glass. He fired again. She kicked him hard with both feet. The door flew open behind her. She flew backward onto the road. Pain shot through her body.

She started to scramble to her feet, but her legs gave way underneath her. She felt back onto the pavement, feeling the blood trickling down her ankle. He'd shot her in the leg.

The General climbed out and walked around the truck toward her.

Then another gunshot split the air. She looked up.

Zack fired as he roared toward them.

Lord, help him. He won't be able to brake!

The General returned fire. The motorcycle grew closer.

Zack was going to hit her. He wouldn't be able to stop in time.

The motorcycle swerved sideways. It skidded. Zack leaped. His body flew through the air as the motorcycle slid down the road and crashed behind him. He hit the ground, rolled twice and then leaped to his feet. The gun was steady in his hands.

"Sorry to crash your vintage motorcycle, sir, but you see, it had no brakes, and I wasn't about to let Rebecca face you alone." He aimed the weapon straight between the General's eyes. "Now drop your weapon, sir."

The General tried to laugh, but the best he could do was splutter. "Stand down, Sergeant. You don't want to go up against me. You'll face a court-martial. Your career will be finished."

Zack tiled his head toward Rebecca. "Can I safely assume you got what you were after, Becs?"

She nodded. Tears filled her eyes. "I did. I got all of it. A full and complete confession."

"Thank You, God." His lips moved in prayer. Then his unrelenting gaze focused hard on the General. "You really should've paid more attention to your daughter, sir. That was quite some business she built in video recording." Anger darkened Zack's smile, but as his eyes darted toward her face, she could see pride filling his eyes. "See, she recorded your whole conversation, and when you're tried and found guilty of attempted murder, the whole world will know that your daughter is the hero who was brave enough to bring you down."

"And conspiracy and treason, Zack," Rebecca said, pulling herself up on her elbows. "He was the leak who was working with Black Talon. And yes, I got it on camera. Every ugly word."

The General spun toward her, ugly, threatening words spilling from his lips.

Zack dived for his chest. One decisive blow and the gun flew from the General's hand. A second blow and the man lay slumped on the pavement, unconscious. Zack reached down and yanked the General's shirt open. There was a small Black Talon tattoo on the top of his chest.

Then Zack turned toward Rebecca. Something soft and tender pooled in his eyes. "You're shot."

"Just my leg, and not that badly." She gritted her teeth. "I'll live."

He lifted her up into his arms and held her tight. She leaned her head against his chest and looked down at the man who had filled her life with such fear.

"But he's right. Even with the recording,

you'll still be court-martialed, for assaulting a superior officer. A decorated hero. You might've just thrown away your military career."

"Maybe." He held her tightly. "Maybe not. Like I said, I have faith in the people I serve with, and I have faith that I'll get through this."

She nestled her head into his chest.

Lord, I love this man. Please, don't let him lose his career over me. Even if that career takes him somewhere far away.

The hard plastic of the hospital waiting room seat dug into Zack's back. He didn't move. It had been six hours since the accident on the highway and the General's treachery had been revealed. Zack's commanding officer had made sure a military escort had reached them before Black Talon could. Now, despite the offer of a ride back to base, Zack had stayed in the hospital while both he and Rebecca gave their statements to police, and Rebecca's leg was stitched up and bandaged. She'd been allowed just twenty minutes alone with the half sister she'd never known she had, before Maria was whisked off in a military helicopter.

Now, he sat with Rebecca curled up into his side while she slept. Her head lay on his chest. His arm wrapped around her shoulder. He was impossibly uncomfortable and dying to stretch. But he didn't move.

"Hey, Zack!" A tall, dark-haired man walked across the waiting room floor.

Zack looked up.

"Mark!" He whispered loudly. He put a finger to his lips and then pointed down at Rebecca. "You made it! How's Katie?"

Mark smiled. His voice dropped to a whisper, too. "She's good. She's pretty tough. It was a bit scary for a while there. But the contractions eventually stopped again and she's under strict instructions to get bed rest for the next couple of weeks. I'm going to stay grounded, too, for the time being. Got to do our best to keep the new little prototype in the workshop a bit longer and avoid a premature launch."

He'd never seen Mark look so tired, exhausted, worried and happy all at once.

"Katie's strong," Zack said. "Just don't let her hear you comparing your new baby to a broadcast unit."

Mark laughed. "Yeah, and you're right, she is strong. She's the best thing that's ever happened to me." He glanced at Rebecca's sleeping form. "Thank you for pushing me to step up and marry her. I had no clue how I was going to balance a relationship, my messed-up, dysfunctional family situation and a job that meant trekking through war zones. But you gave me the kick I needed. You made me see I was willing to take the risk. I don't know if I ever thanked you for that or returned the favor."

He could tell Mark was being sincere. But he also knew his buddy well enough to know that Mark was trying to return the favor right here and now in the hospital waiting room. He didn't need Mark's relationship advice. Zack already knew full well that Rebecca was incredible. He just didn't know how they could possibly have a life together.

"What you and Katie have works because you travel together most of the time," Zack said. "With Rebecca it would be different. I would hardly be able to take her with me on deployment. I would disappear from her life on short notice and not be able to tell her where I was going, or fill her in on everything that happened when I got home."

Mark waved a hand at him to stop. But Zack kept talking.

"Yes, I love her." Zack's voice rose. "I adore her. I'm impressed by her and challenged by her. I'm crazy about her."

Mark raised an eyebrow. "Chill. Relax. Just—"

"I'm tired of chilling and relaxing." Zack

groaned. "Saying goodbye to her is going to kill me. Do I want to marry her? Yes. Of course I do. But I'm not going to put her through a life that she doesn't want."

Rebecca shifted in his arms. Zack looked down. She sat up slowly in his arms.

Out of the corner of his eye, Zack could see a man in military uniform stepping in the front door—Major Jeff Lyons, his commanding officer, was here. Mark crossed over to speak to him.

Rebecca's eyes were on his face. What had she heard? It didn't matter. All that mattered was that he'd said it and he meant it. Zack took Rebecca's hands in his.

"I'm in love with you, Becs. I've always been in love with you. Ever since that first moment I looked across the gym and came face-to-face with the most beautiful person I've ever laid eyes on. You're strong. You're smart. You're amazing." His eyes glanced at his commanding officer. "I wish we could be together forever."

"Sergeant, need another minute?" Jeff called, in a tone of voice that implied there were no spare moments to be had.

"One second." He turned back to Rebecca. "Could you spend the rest of your life with a soldier? Could you spend the rest of your life loving a man who's going to disappear for weeks and months at a time?"

"I don't know." Her eyes met his. "I honestly don't."

He nodded. Okay. That was fair enough. He'd asked her an honest question. She'd given him an honest answer. What more could he ask for?

He pulled back. He had to go. Their time together was over.

But her hands slipped around his neck.

"But I know that I love you, too," she said. "I always have, and I know that I want us to try."

Hope exploded in his heart. He gathered her into his arms and kissed her, as if his heart, mind and body were holding on to her with everything they had. He felt her hands running through his hair and the curve of her body melting into his.

Major Jeff Lyons coughed politely. Zack pulled back.

"I won't lose you again, I promise." He stood up. "I'll write to you. I'll visit you. I'll find you." A smile lit up her lips. He walked backward toward the doorway, feeling his heart pull back toward her with every step. "I won't let you go, ever again. I promise. I will love you, Rebecca Miles."

"You'd better!" she called.

He stepped out of the hospital waiting room and followed his commanding officer out into the sunlight.

EPILOGUE

Rebecca braced her legs against the dusty soil, tucked a wisp of hair back into her bandanna and slowly swung the camera's gaze over the wide expanse of North African wilderness. The sun beat down heavily on the back of her neck. Heat rose up around her in shimmering waves. She focused her lens on the small family nestled together in a dip in the valley below.

Katie's golden hair shimmered in the unrelenting sun. Mark's arm lay firmly around her waist. Katie slid six-month-old Noah out of a chest carrier and into his father's waiting arms. Then she turned and started down the valley toward the women's co-op, to give a workshop on the new well system Shield Trust was building.

A motorcycle rumbled in the distance. Shivers ran down Rebecca's neck. It had been seven months since she'd last set eyes on Sergeant Zachary Keats. But the sound of a motorcycle still set off sparklers down her spine. Between his work and her new project with Katie and Mark's charity, she and Zack had barely ever been on the same continent, let alone in the same country.

But they'd written. Oh, how they'd written. Emails and texts and long handwritten letters. About clearing his name and getting back out onto the field. About the criminal charges the disgraced General was facing and the attempts authorities were now making to dismantle the foothold Black Talon had gotten in Canada. Seth's mother's grave had been found, thanks to a tip from Dmitry, who'd been all too eager to turn on the General. Seth and Maria had both pled guilty, but hadn't given up the hope of tracking down other siblings they might have around the world.

And through it all, Zack and Rebecca had written about their dreams for the future and their hopes it would include being together.

The motorcycle grew closer. She panned the camera down to get a better look.

Broad shoulders. Strong arms.

He hit the brakes and slid his visor up. Her eyes fell on the rugged face and gentle smile of the man who set every corner of her heart on fire.

She ran down the sand toward him. Zack

leaped off the motorcycle, yanked off his helmet and ran for her. He caught her halfway up the hill. His strong arms lifted her up off the ground.

"What are you doing here?" she said. "I thought you weren't getting leave for a month?"

He set her down. "I'm stationed at a base a few miles from here. I got a day pass. And when I heard from Mark that you were going to be here this week, too, I couldn't wait a moment longer for this."

"For what?"

Zack dropped to one knee in the sand.

"Marry me, Rebecca." He pulled a handmade ring out of his back pocket, of twisted copper and silver wire twisted into a smooth, intricate circle. "Be my partner. Be my wife. I'm sorry I didn't have time to buy a ring, and I know we've talked about it. But I don't want to wait. I want us to know that no matter where we are in the world, our home is each other."

"Yes." She was laughing so hard she was almost crying. She held out her hand and let him slide the ring onto her finger. "You know I want to marry you—"

"Are you sure this is what you want?" His fingers hovered over hers. "To spend your life married to a military man? I've put in for a transfer for a job back at headquarters. Which means I'll be able to come home to you every night and we'll be able to build a real life together, Becs. Having been on the front line of discovering how Black Talon had infiltrated North America, I want to be involved in the fight to take them down."

"I wouldn't have it any other way." Her hands brushed his face. "You'll save lives. I'll tell stories. And we'll both always come home to each other. So, yes, I will marry you."

He slid the ring on her finger. "But would you marry me today?"

"Today?"

"Today." Zack stood. He took her hands in both of his. "I'm shipping out of here tomorrow morning. I want to marry you today. This afternoon. Elope with me. With the base chaplain performing the ceremony, and Katie and Mark as our witnesses."

She took a deep breath and felt her heart rising inside her chest. The sun rose high in the blue sky above her. Joy filled her heart and sparkled in her eyes.

"If you want me to wait, a year, five years, ten more years to make you my wife, I will," Zack added. "I promise I will wait for you, no matter how long it takes. We can wait until we've saved up for a dress, and a banquet, and—"

She shook her head. "No."

He stopped. “No?”

She smiled. “No, you don’t have to wait a moment longer. Yes, Zack, yes, I will marry you today. Right now. I don’t need a fancy dress. I don’t need a banquet. I just need you. You’re all I’ve ever needed. Just you. And I can’t wait to start our life together.”

His eyes rose to the sky. “Thank You, Lord.” Then his eyes met hers again. “Trust me, it’s not always easy to be a patient man.”

She laughed. Her hands slipped around his neck. His strong arms encircled her. Her lips kissed his deeply. Then he carried her down the hill to his bike.

* * * * *

Dear Reader,

When *Killer Assignment* came out in 2013, I received a letter from a reader asking me to write a book about Mark's friend Zack. She wanted to find out more about the steady, unflappable military man who'd come to Mark and Katie's rescue.

Most of all, this wonderful reader asked me to help Zack find the love of his life—which was an interesting challenge. Rebecca was a fun and fascinating character to get to know and I think she suits Zack perfectly. I hope you think so, too. Plus, it was great fun to be able to catch up with Mark and Katie, too.

Growing up around the world, I was fortunate to get to know several military families, and to spend time with people who've served in the American, British and Canadian militaries. Their dedication and determination inspired me, as did the strength of their families.

While there are several decommissioned military bases dotting Canada, the base at Remi Lake is entirely fictional, as are some of the details surrounding the Canadian special ops. I'm very thankful for my history buff husband for helping me fill in many of the details in this book. I think he's always been waiting for me to create a special ops hero!

Thanks to you, too, for sharing Zack and Rebecca's story with me. If you want to get in touch, you can visit me at www.maggiekblack.com or follow me, @maggiekblack on Twitter.

As always, thank you for sharing the journey,
Maggie